Dover Thrift

Macbeth

WILLIAM SHAKESPEARE

DOVER PUBLICATIONS, INC.
Mineola, New York

Bibliographical Note

This Dover edition, first published in 2009, contains the unabridged text of *Macbeth,* as published in Volume II of the second edition of *The Works of William Shakespeare,* Macmillan and Co., London, 1892, plus literary analysis and perspectives from *MAXnotes® for Macbeth,* published in 2004 by Research & Education Association, Inc., Piscataway, New Jersey. The explanatory footnotes to the text of the play were prepared for the present edition.

Library of Congress Cataloging-in-Publication Data

Shakespeare, William, 1564–1616.
   Macbeth : thrift study edition / William Shakespeare.
     p. cm.
   ISBN-13: 978-0-486-47575-2
   ISBN-10: 0-486-47575-1
   1. Macbeth, King of Scotland, 11th cent.—Drama. 2. Scotland—Kings and rulers—Drama. 3. Regicides—Drama. 4. Shakespeare, William, 1564–1616. Macbeth. I. Title.

PR2823.A2D68 2009
822.3'3—dc22

2009024682

Manufactured in the United States by Courier Corporation
47575104   2013
www.doverpublications.com

Publisher's Note

Combining the complete text of a classic novel or drama with a comprehensive study guide, Dover Thrift Study Editions are the most effective way to gain a thorough understanding of the major works of world literature.

The study guide features up-to-date and expert analysis of every chapter or section from the source work. Questions and fully explained answers follow, allowing readers to analyze the material critically. Character lists, author bios, and discussions of the work's historical context are also provided.

Each Dover Thrift Study Edition includes everything a student needs to prepare for homework, discussions, reports, and exams.

Contents

Macbeth v

Study Guide 83

Macbeth

WILLIAM SHAKESPEARE

Contents

Dramatis Personæ viii
Act I 1
    Scene I 1
    Scene II 1
    Scene III 4
    Scene IV 9
    Scene V 11
    Scene VI 14
    Scene VII 15
Act II 19
    Scene I 19
    Scene II 21
    Scene III 24
    Scene IV 29
Act III 33
    Scene I 33
    Scene II 38
    Scene III 40
    Scene IV 41
    Scene V 46
    Scene VI 47
Act IV 51
    Scene I 51
    Scene II 56
    Scene III 59
Act V 69
    Scene I 69
    Scene II 71
    Scene III 72
    Scene IV 75
    Scene V 76
    Scene VI 78
    Scene VII 78
    Scene VIII 80

Dramatis Personæ

DUNCAN, king of Scotland
MALCOLM, } his sons.
DONALBAIN,

MACBETH, } generals of the King's army.
BANQUO,

MACDUFF,
LENNOX,
ROSS,
MENTEITH, } noblemen of Scotland.
ANGUS,
CAITHNESS,
FLEANCE, son to Banquo.
SIWARD, Earl of Northumberland, general of the English forces.
YOUNG SIWARD, his son.
SEYTON, an officer attending on Macbeth.
BOY, son to Macduff.
An English Doctor.
A Scotch Doctor.
A Sergeant.
A Porter.
An Old Man.

Lady MACBETH.
Lady MACDUFF.
Gentlewoman attending on Lady Macbeth.

HECATE.
Three Witches.
Apparitions.

Lords, Gentlemen, Officers, Soldiers, Murderers, Attendants, and Messengers.

SCENE: *Scotland; England.*

ACT I.

SCENE I. *A desert place.*

Thunder and lightning. Enter three Witches.

FIRST WITCH.　　When shall we three meet again
　　　　In thunder, lightning, or in rain?
SEC. WITCH.　　When the hurlyburly's done,
　　　　When the battle's lost and won.
THIRD WITCH.　　That will be ere the set of sun.
FIRST WITCH.　　Where the place?
SEC. WITCH.　　　　　　　　Upon the heath.
THIRD WITCH.　　There to meet with Macbeth.
FIRST WITCH.　　I come, Graymalkin.[1]
ALL.　　Paddock[2] calls:—anon!
　　　　Fair is foul, and foul is fair.
　　　　Hover through the fog and filthy air.　　　　　[*Exeunt.*

SCENE II. *A camp near Forres.*

Alarum within. Enter DUNCAN, MALCOLM, DONALBAIN, LENNOX, *with* Attendants, *meeting a bleeding* Sergeant.

DUN.　　What bloody man is that? He can report,
　　　　As seemeth by his plight, of the revolt
　　　　The newest state.

---

[1] *Graymalkin*] a witches' familiar in the shape of a cat.
[2] *Paddock*] a toad (another witches' familiar).

1

MAL.   This is the sergeant
Who like a good and hardy soldier fought
'Gainst my captivity. Hail, brave friend!
Say to the king the knowledge of the broil
As thou didst leave it.

SER.   Doubtful it stood;
As two spent swimmers, that do cling together
And choke their art. The merciless Macdonwald—
Worthy to be a rebel, for to that
The multiplying villanies of nature
Do swarm upon him—from the western isles
Of kerns and gallowglasses[1] is supplied;
And fortune, on his damned quarrel smiling,
Show'd like a rebel's whore: but all's too weak:
For brave Macbeth—well he deserves that name—
Disdaining fortune, with his brandish'd steel,
Which smoked with bloody execution,
Like valour's minion carved out his passage
Till he faced the slave;
Which ne'er shook hands, nor bade farewell to him,
Till he unseam'd him from the nave to the chaps,[2]
And fix'd his head upon our battlements.

DUN.   O valiant cousin! worthy gentleman!

SER.   As whence the sun 'gins his reflection
Shipwrecking storms and direful thunders break,
So from that spring whence comfort seem'd to come
Discomfort swells. Mark, king of Scotland, mark:
No sooner justice had, with valour arm'd,
Compell'd these skipping kerns to trust their heels,
But the Norweyan lord, surveying vantage,[3]
With furbish'd arms and new supplies of men,
Began a fresh assault.

DUN.   Dismay'd not this
Our captains, Macbeth and Banquo?

SER.   Yes;
As sparrows eagles, or the hare the lion.

---

[1] *kerns and gallowglasses*] Irish foot soldiers.
[2] *nave to the chaps*] navel to the jaw.
[3] *surveying vantage*] seeing his opportunity.

If I say sooth, I must report they were
As cannons overcharged with double cracks;
So they
Doubly redoubled strokes upon the foe:
Except they meant to bathe in reeking wounds,
Or memorize another Golgotha,[4]
I cannot tell—
But I am faint; my gashes cry for help.

DUN.   So well thy words become thee as thy wounds;
They smack of honour both. Go get him surgeons.
                                [*Exit Sergeant, attended.*

Who comes here?

Enter ROSS.

MAL.   The worthy thane of Ross.
LEN.   What a haste looks through his eyes! So should he look
That seems to speak things strange.
ROSS.   God save the king!
DUN.   Whence camest thou, worthy thane?
ROSS.   From Fife, great king;
Where the Norweyan banners flout the sky
And fan our people cold.
Norway himself, with terrible numbers,
Assisted by that most disloyal traitor
The thane of Cawdor, began a dismal[5] conflict;
Till that Bellona's[6] bridegroom, lapp'd in proof,[7]
Confronted him with self-comparisons,[8]
Point against point rebellious, arm 'gainst arm,
Curbing his lavish spirit: and, to conclude,
The victory fell on us.
DUN.   Great happiness!
ROSS.   That now
Sweno, the Norways' king, craves composition;[9]

---

[4] *Golgotha*] the place of execution outside Jerusalem; also known as Calvary.
[5] *dismal*] fatal.
[6] *Bellona*] goddess of war.
[7] *lapp'd in proof*] clad in impenetrable armor.
[8] *self-comparisons*] equal force and skill.
[9] *composition*] accord, peace.

                Nor would we deign him burial of his men
                Till he disbursed, at Saint Colme's inch, [10]
                Ten thousand dollars to our general use.
DUN.   No more that thane of Cawdor shall deceive
                Our bosom interest: go pronounce his present death,
                And with his former title greet Macbeth.
ROSS.   I'll see it done.
DUN.   What he hath lost, noble Macbeth hath won.   [*Exeunt.*

SCENE III. *A heath.*

Thunder. Enter the three Witches.

FIRST WITCH.   Where hast thou been, sister?
SEC. WITCH.   Killing swine.
THIRD WITCH.   Sister, where thou?
FIRST WITCH.   A sailor's wife had chestnuts in her lap,
                And mounch'd, [1] and mounch'd, and mounch'd. 'Give me,'
                    quoth I:
                'Aroint thee, [2] witch!' the rump-fed ronyon [3] cries.
                Her husband's to Aleppo gone, master o' the Tiger:
                But in a sieve I'll thither sail,
                And, like a rat without a tail,
                I'll do, I'll do, and I'll do.
SEC. WITCH.   I'll give thee a wind.
FIRST WITCH.   Thou'rt kind.
THIRD WITCH.   And I another.
FIRST WITCH.   I myself have all the other;
                And the very ports they blow,
                All the quarters that they know
                I' the shipman's card. [4]
                I will drain him dry as hay:

---

[10] *inch*] island.
[1] *mounch'd*] munched.
[2] *Aroint thee*] begone.
[3] *ronyon*] mangy creature.
[4] *shipman's card*] compass or chart.

        Sleep shall neither night nor day
        Hang upon his pent-house lid;[5]
        He shall live a man forbid:
        Weary se'nnights nine times nine
        Shall he dwindle, peak,[6] and pine:
        Though his bark cannot be lost,
        Yet it shall be tempest-tost.
        Look what I have.

SEC. WITCH.   Show me, show me.

FIRST WITCH.   Here I have a pilot's thumb,
        Wreck'd as homeward he did come.   [*Drum within.*

THIRD WITCH.   A drum, a drum!
        Macbeth doth come.

ALL.   The weird sisters, hand in hand,
        Posters[7] of the sea and land,
        Thus do go about, about:
        Thrice to thine, and thrice to mine,
        And thrice again, to make up nine.
        Peace! the charm's wound up.

Enter MACBETH *and* BANQUO.

MACB.   So foul and fair a day I have not seen.

BAN.   How far is't call'd to Forres? What are these
        So wither'd, and so wild in their attire,
        That look not like the inhabitants o' the earth,
        And yet are on't? Live you? or are you aught
        That man may question? You seem to understand me,
        By each at once her choppy[8] finger laying
        Upon her skinny lips: you should be women,
        And yet your beards forbid me to interpret
        That you are so.

MACB.   Speak, if you can: what are you?

FIRST WITCH.   All hail, Macbeth! hail to thee, thane of Glamis!

SEC. WITCH.   All hail, Macbeth! hail to thee, thane of Cawdor!

---

[5] *pent-house lid*] eyelid.
[6] *peak*] grow thin.
[7] *Posters*] swift travelers.
[8] *choppy*] chapped.

THIRD WITCH.   All hail, Macbeth, that shalt be king hereafter!
BAN.   Good sir, why do you start, and seem to fear
    Things that do sound so fair? I' the name of truth,
    Are ye fantastical,[9] or that indeed
    Which outwardly ye show? My noble partner
    You greet with present grace and great prediction
    Of noble having[10] and of royal hope,
    That he seems rapt withal: to me you speak not:
    If you can look into the seeds of time,
    And say which grain will grow and which will not,
    Speak then to me, who neither beg nor fear
    Your favours nor your hate.
FIRST WITCH.   Hail!
SEC. WITCH.   Hail!
THIRD WITCH.   Hail!
FIRST WITCH.   Lesser than Macbeth, and greater.
SEC. WITCH.   Not so happy, yet much happier.
THIRD WITCH.   Thou shalt get kings, though thou be none:
    So all hail, Macbeth and Banquo!
FIRST WITCH.   Banquo and Macbeth, all hail!
MACB.   Stay, you imperfect speakers, tell me more:
    By Sinel's death I know I am thane of Glamis;
    But how of Cawdor? the thane of Cawdor lives,
    A prosperous gentleman; and to be king
    Stands not within the prospect of belief,
    No more than to be Cawdor. Say from whence
    You owe[11] this strange intelligence? or why
    Upon this blasted heath you stop our way
    With such prophetic greeting? Speak, I charge you.
                [*Witches vanish.*
BAN.   The earth hath bubbles as the water has,
    And these are of them: whither are they vanish'd?
MACB.   Into the air, and what seem'd corporal melted
    As breath into the wind. Would they had stay'd!
BAN.   Were such things here as we do speak about?

---

[9] *fantastical*] imaginary.
[10] *having*] estate, property.
[11] *owe*] possess.

	Or have we eaten on the insane root
	That takes the reason prisoner?
MACB.	Your children shall be kings.
BAN.	You shall be king.
MACB.	And thane of Cawdor too: went it not so?
BAN.	To the selfsame tune and words. Who's here?

Enter ROSS *and* ANGUS.

ROSS. The king hath happily received, Macbeth,
The news of thy success: and when he reads
Thy personal venture in the rebels' fight,
His wonders and his praises do contend
Which should be thine or his: silenced with that,
In viewing o'er the rest o' the selfsame day,
He finds thee in the stout Norweyan ranks,
Nothing afeard of what thyself didst make,
Strange images of death. As thick as hail
Came post with post, and every one did bear
Thy praises in his kingdom's great defence,
And pour'd them down before him.

ANG.   We are sent
To give thee, from our royal master, thanks;
Only to herald thee into his sight,
Not pay thee.

ROSS. And for an earnest[12] of a greater honour,
He bade me, from him, call thee thane of Cawdor:
In which addition,[13] hail, most worthy thane!
For it is thine.

BAN.   What, can the devil speak true?

MACB. The thane of Cawdor lives: why do you dress me
In borrow'd robes?

ANG.   Who was the thane lives yet,
But under heavy judgement bears that life
Which he deserves to lose. Whether he was combined
With those of Norway, or did line[14] the rebel
With hidden help and vantage, or that with both

---

[12] *earnest*] portion paid as a pledge.
[13] *addition*] title.
[14] *line*] strengthen.

He labour'd in his country's wreck, I know not;
But treasons capital, confess'd and proved,
Have overthrown him.

MACB.   [*Aside*] Glamis, and thane of Cawdor:
The greatest is behind.—Thanks for your pains.—
Do you not hope your children shall be kings,
When those that gave the thane of Cawdor to me
Promised no less to them?

BAN.   That, trusted home,
Might yet enkindle you unto the crown,
Besides the thane of Cawdor. But 'tis strange:
And oftentimes, to win us to our harm,
The instruments of darkness tell us truths,
Win us with honest trifles, to betray's
In deepest consequence.
Cousins, a word, I pray you.

MACB.   [*Aside*] Two truths are told,
As happy prologues to the swelling act
Of the imperial theme.—I thank you, gentlemen.—
[*Aside*] This supernatural soliciting
Cannot be ill; cannot be good: if ill,
Why hath it given me earnest of success,
Commencing in a truth? I am thane of Cawdor:
If good, why do I yield to that suggestion
Whose horrid image doth unfix my hair
And make my seated heart knock at my ribs,
Against the use of nature? Present fears
Are less than horrible imaginings:
My thought, whose murder yet is but fantastical,
Shakes so my single state of man that function
Is smother'd in surmise, and nothing is
But what is not.

BAN.   Look, how our partner's rapt.

MACB. [*Aside*] If chance will have me king, why, chance may crown
     me,
Without my stir.

BAN.   New honours come upon him,
Like our strange garments, cleave not to their mould
But with the aid of use.

MACB.   [*Aside*] Come what come may,

        Time and the hour runs through the roughest day.

BAN.   Worthy Macbeth, we stay upon your leisure.

MACB.   Give me your favour:[15] my dull brain was wrought
        With things forgotten. Kind gentlemen, your pains
        Are register'd where every day I turn
        The leaf to read them. Let us toward the king.
        Think upon what hath chanced, and at more time,
        The interim having weigh'd it, let us speak
        Our free hearts each to other.

BAN.   Very gladly.

MACB.   Till then, enough. Come, friends.   *[Exeunt.*

SCENE IV. *Forres. The palace.*

Flourish. Enter DUNCAN, MALCOLM, DONALBAIN, LENNOX, *and* Attendants.

DUN.   Is execution done on Cawdor? Are not
        Those in commission yet return'd?

MAL.   My liege,
        They are not yet come back. But I have spoke
        With one that saw him die, who did report
        That very frankly he confess'd his treasons,
        Implored your highness' pardon and set forth
        A deep repentance: nothing in his life
        Became him like the leaving it; he died
        As one that had been studied in his death,
        To throw away the dearest thing he owed
        As 'twere a careless trifle.

DUN.   There's no art
        To find the mind's construction in the face:
        He was a gentleman on whom I built
        An absolute trust.

[15] *favour]* pardon.

Enter MACBETH, BANQUO, ROSS, *and* ANGUS.

O worthiest cousin!

The sin of my ingratitude even now
Was heavy on me: thou art so far before,
That swiftest wing of recompense is slow
To overtake thee. Would thou hadst less deserved,
That the proportion both of thanks and payment
Might have been mine! only I have left to say,
More is thy due than more than all can pay.

MACB. The service and the loyalty I owe,
In doing it, pays itself. Your highness' part
Is to receive our duties: and our duties
Are to your throne and state children and servants;
Which do but what they should, by doing every thing
Safe toward[1] your love and honour.

DUN.   Welcome hither:
I have begun to plant thee, and will labour
To make thee full of growing. Noble Banquo,
That hast no less deserved, nor must be known
No less to have done so: let me infold thee
And hold thee to my heart.

BAN.   There if I grow,
The harvest is your own.

DUN.   My plenteous joys,
Wanton in fulness, seek to hide themselves
In drops of sorrow. Sons, kinsmen, thanes,
And you whose places are the nearest, know,
We will establish our estate upon
Our eldest, Malcolm, whom we name hereafter
The Prince of Cumberland: which honour must
Not unaccompanied invest him only,
But signs of nobleness, like stars, shall shine
On all deservers. From hence to Inverness,
And bind us further to you.

MACB. The rest is labour, which is not used for you:
I'll be myself the harbinger, and make joyful
The hearing of my wife with your approach;

---

[1] *Safe toward*] to secure (or consistent with).

So humbly take my leave.

DUN.   My worthy Cawdor!

MACB.   [*Aside*] The Prince of Cumberland! that is a step
On which I must fall down, or else o'erleap,
For in my way it lies. Stars, hide your fires;
Let not light see my black and deep desires:
The eye wink at the hand; yet let that be
Which the eye fears, when it is done, to see.   [*Exit.*

DUN.   True, worthy Banquo; he is full so valiant,
And in his commendations I am fed;
It is a banquet to me. Let's after him,
Whose care is gone before to bid us welcome:
It is a peerless kinsman.   [*Flourish. Exeunt.*

SCENE V. *Inverness. Macbeth's castle.*

Enter LADY MACBETH, *reading a letter.*

LADY M. 'They met me in the day of success; and I have learned by the
perfectest report, they have more in them than mortal knowledge.
When I burned in desire to question them further, they made themselves air, into which they vanished. Whiles I stood rapt in the wonder
of it, came missives[1] from the king, who all-hailed me "Thane of
Cawdor"; by which title, before, these weird sisters saluted me, and
referred me to the coming on of time, with "Hail, king that shalt be!"
This have I thought good to deliver thee, my dearest partner of
greatness, that thou mightst not lose the dues of rejoicing, by being
ignorant of what greatness is promised thee. Lay it to thy heart, and
farewell.'

Glamis thou art, and Cawdor, and shalt be
What thou art promised: yet do I fear thy nature;
It is too full o' the milk of human kindness
To catch the nearest way: thou wouldst be great;
Art not without ambition, but without

---

[1] *missives*] messengers.

The illness[2] should attend it: what thou wouldst highly,
That wouldst thou holily; wouldst not play false,
And yet wouldst wrongly win: thou 'ldst have, great Glamis,
That which cries 'Thus thou must do, if thou have it;
And that which rather thou dost fear to do
Than wishest should be undone.' Hie thee hither,
That I may pour my spirits in thine ear,
And chastise with the valour of my tongue
All that impedes thee from the golden round,
Which fate and metaphysical[3] aid doth seem
To have thee crown'd withal.

Enter a MESSENGER.

                        What is your tidings?

MESS. The king comes here to-night.

LADY M.   Thou'rt mad to say it:
Is not thy master with him? who, were't so,
Would have inform'd for preparation.

MESS. So please you, it is true: our thane is coming:
One of my fellows had the speed of him,
Who, almost dead for breath, had scarcely more
Than would make up his message.

LADY M.   Give him tending;
He brings great news.   *[Exit Messenger.*
                The raven himself is hoarse
That croaks the fatal entrance of Duncan
Under my battlements. Come, you spirits
That tend on mortal[4] thoughts, unsex me here,
And fill me, from the crown to the toe, top-full
Of direst cruelty! make thick my blood,
Stop up the access and passage to remorse,[5]
That no compunctious visitings of nature
Shake my fell purpose, nor keep peace between
The effect and it! Come to my woman's breasts,

---

[2] *illness*] wickedness.
[3] *metaphysical*] supernatural.
[4] *mortal*] deadly, murderous.
[5] *remorse*] pity, tenderness.

And take[6] my milk for gall, you murdering ministers,
Wherever in your sightless[7] substances
You wait on nature's mischief! Come, thick night,
And pall thee in the dunnest smoke of hell,
That my keen knife see not the wound it makes,
Nor heaven peep through the blanket of the dark,
To cry 'Hold, hold!'

Enter MACBETH.

                               Great Glamis! worthy Cawdor!
Greater than both, by the all-hail hereafter!
Thy letters have transported me beyond
This ignorant present, and I feel now
The future in the instant.

MACB.   My dearest love,
Duncan comes here to-night.

LADY M.   And when goes hence?

MACB.   To-morrow, as he purposes.

LADY M.   O, never
Shall sun that morrow see!
Your face, my thane, is as a book where men
May read strange matters. To beguile the time,[8]
Look like the time; bear welcome in your eye,
Your hand, your tongue: look like the innocent flower,
But be the serpent under't. He that's coming
Must be provided for: and you shall put
This night's great business into my dispatch;
Which shall to all our nights and days to come
Give solely sovereign sway and masterdom.

MACB.   We will speak further.

LADY M.   Only look up clear;
To alter favour[9] ever is to fear:
Leave all the rest to me.   [*Exeunt.*

---

[6] *take*] exchange.
[7] *sightless*] invisible.
[8] *time*] world, others.
[9] *favour*] expression, countenance.

SCENE VI. *Before Macbeth's castle.*

Hautboys and torches. Enter DUNCAN, MALCOLM, DONALBAIN, BAN-QUO, LENNOX, MACDUFF, ROSS, ANGUS, *and* Attendants.

DUN.   This castle hath a pleasant seat; the air
      Nimbly and sweetly recommends itself
      Unto our gentle senses.

BAN.   This guest of summer,
      The temple-haunting martlet,[1] does approve[2]
      By his loved mansionry that the heaven's breath
      Smells wooingly here: no jutty,[3] frieze,
      Buttress, nor coign[4] of vantage, but this bird
      Hath made his pendent bed and procreant cradle:
      Where they most breed and haunt, I have observed
      The air is delicate.

Enter LADY MACBETH.

DUN.   See, see, our honour'd hostess!
      The love that follows us sometime is our trouble,
      Which still we thank as love. Herein I teach you
      How you shall bid God 'ild[5] us for your pains,
      And thank us for your trouble.

LADY M.   All our service
      In every point twice done, and then done double,
      Were poor and single business to contend
      Against those honours deep and broad wherewith
      Your majesty loads our house: for those of old,
      And the late dignities heap'd up to them,
      We rest your hermits.[6]

DUN.   Where's the thane of Cawdor?
      We coursed him at the heels, and had a purpose

---

[1] *martlet*] house-martin.
[2] *approve*] prove.
[3] *jutty*] projection.
[4] *coign*] corner.
[5] *'ild*] reward.
[6] *hermits*] beadsmen, those who pray for another.

To be his purveyor:[7] but he rides well,
And his great love, sharp as his spur, hath holp him
To his home before us. Fair and noble hostess,
We are your guest to-night.

LADY M.   Your servants ever
Have theirs, themselves, and what is theirs, in compt,[8]
To make their audit at your highness' pleasure,
Still to return your own.

DUN.   Give me your hand;
Conduct me to mine host: we love him highly,
And shall continue our graces towards him.
By your leave, hostess.   [*Exeunt.*

SCENE VII. *Macbeth's castle.*

Hautboys and torches. Enter a Sewer,[1] *and divers* Servants *with dishes
and service, and pass over the stage. Then enter* MACBETH.

MACB.   If it were done when 'tis done, then 'twere well
It were done quickly: if the assassination
Could trammel up[2] the consequence, and catch,
With his surcease,[3] success; that but this blow
Might be the be-all and the end-all here,
But here, upon this bank and shoal of time,
We'ld jump the life to come. But in these cases
We still have judgement here; that we but teach
Bloody instructions, which being taught return
To plague the inventor: this even-handed justice
Commends the ingredients of our poison'd chalice
To our own lips. He's here in double trust:
First, as I am his kinsman and his subject,

---

[7] *purveyor*] provider.
[8] *compt*] account.

---

[1] *Sewer*] head servant.
[2] *trammel up*] tie up or catch in a net.
[3] *surcease*] death.

Strong both against the deed; then, as his host,
Who should against his murderer shut the door,
Not bear the knife myself. Besides, this Duncan
Hath borne his faculties[4] so meek, hath been
So clear[5] in his great office, that his virtues
Will plead like angels trumpet-tongued against
The deep damnation of his taking-off;
And pity, like a naked new-born babe,
Striding[6] the blast, or heaven's cherubin horsed
Upon the sightless couriers of the air,
Shall blow the horrid deed in every eye,
That tears shall drown the wind. I have no spur
To prick the sides of my intent, but only
Vaulting ambition, which o'erleaps itself
And falls on the other.[7]

Enter LADY MACBETH.

                             How now! what news?
LADY M. He has almost supp'd: why have you left the chamber?
MACB.   Hath he ask'd for me?
LADY M.   Know you not he has?
MACB.   We will proceed no further in this business:
         He hath honour'd me of late; and I have bought
         Golden opinions from all sorts of people,
         Which would be worn now in their newest gloss,
         Not cast aside so soon.
LADY M.   Was the hope drunk
         Wherein you dress'd yourself? hath it slept since?
         And wakes it now, to look so green and pale
         At what it did so freely? From this time
         Such I account thy love. Art thou afeard
         To be the same in thine own act and valour
         As thou art in desire? Wouldst thou have that
         Which thou esteem'st the ornament of life,
         And live a coward in thine own esteem,

---

[4] *faculties*] powers.
[5] *clear*] irreproachable.
[6] *Striding*] bestriding, mounting.
[7] *other*] other side (of the horse).

    Letting 'I dare not' wait upon 'I would,'
    Like the poor cat i' the adage?

MACB.   Prithee, peace:
    I dare do all that may become a man;
    Who dares do more is none.

LADY M.   What beast was't then
    That made you break this enterprise to me?
    When you durst do it, then you were a man;
    And, to be more than what you were, you would
    Be so much more the man. Nor time 'nor place
    Did then adhere, and yet you would make both:
    They have made themselves, and that their fitness now
    Does unmake you. I have given suck, and know
    How tender 'tis to love the babe that milks me:
    I would, while it was smiling in my face,
    Have pluck'd my nipple from his boneless gums,
    And dash'd the brains out, had I so sworn as you
    Have done to this.

MACB.   If we should fail?

LADY M.   We fail!
    But screw your courage to the sticking-place,
    And we'll not fail. When Duncan is asleep—
    Whereto the rather shall his day's hard journey
    Soundly invite him—his two chamberlains
    Will I with wine and wassail so convince,[8]
    That memory, the warder of the brain,
    Shall be a fume, and the receipt of reason
    A limbec[9] only: when in swinish sleep
    Their drenched natures lie as in a death,
    What cannot you and I perform upon
    The unguarded Duncan? what not put upon
    His spongy officers, who shall bear the guilt
    Of our great quell?[10]

MACB.   Bring forth men-children only;
    For thy undaunted mettle should compose
    Nothing but males. Will it not be received,

---

[8] *convince*] overcome.
[9] *limbec*] alembic, still.
[10] *quell*] murder.

When we have mark'd with blood those sleepy two
Of his own chamber, and used their very daggers,
That they have done't?

LADY M.   Who dares receive it other,
As we shall make our griefs and clamour roar
Upon his death?

MACB.   I am settled, and bend up
Each corporal agent to this terrible feat.
Away, and mock the time with fairest show:
False face must hide what the false heart doth know. [*Exeunt.*

ACT II.

Scene I. *Inverness. Court of Macbeth's castle.*

Enter Banquo, *and* Fleance *bearing a torch before him.*

Ban.   How goes the night, boy?
Fle.   The moon is down; I have not heard the clock.
Ban.   And she goes down at twelve.
Fle.   I take't, 'tis later, sir.
Ban.   Hold, take my sword. There's husbandry in heaven,
        Their candles are all out. Take thee that too.
        A heavy summons lies like lead upon me,
        And yet I would not sleep. Merciful powers,
        Restrain in me the cursed thoughts that nature
        Gives way to in repose!

Enter Macbeth, *and a* Servant *with a torch.*

                    Give me my sword.
        Who's there?
Macb.   A friend.
Ban.   What, sir, not yet at rest? The king's a-bed:
        He hath been in unusual pleasure, and
        Sent forth great largess to your offices:[1]
        This diamond he greets your wife withal,
        By the name of most kind hostess; and shut up
        In measureless content.
Macb.   Being unprepared,
        Our will became the servant to defect,
        Which else should free have wrought.
Ban.   All's well.

---

[1] *offices*] servants' quarters.

19

   I dreamt last night of the three weird sisters:
   To you they have show'd some truth.
MACB.   I think not of them:
   Yet, when we can entreat an hour to serve,
   We would spend it in some words upon that business,
   If you would grant the time.
BAN.   At your kind'st leisure.
MACB. If you shall cleave to my consent, when 'tis,
   It shall make honour for you.
BAN.   So I lose none
   In seeking to augment it, but still keep
   My bosom franchised and allegiance clear,
   I shall be counsell'd.
MACB.   Good repose the while!
BAN. Thanks, sir: the like to you! [*Exeunt Banquo and Fleance.*
MACB. Go bid thy mistress, when my drink is ready,
   She strike upon the bell. Get thee to bed. [*Exit Servant.*
   Is this a dagger which I see before me,
   The handle toward my hand? Come, let me clutch thee.
   I have thee not, and yet I see thee still.
   Art thou not, fatal vision, sensible
   To feeling as to sight? or art thou but
   A dagger of the mind, a false creation,
   Proceeding from the heat-oppressed brain?
   I see thee yet, in form as palpable
   As this which now I draw.
   Thou marshall'st me the way that I was going;
   And such an instrument I was to use.
   Mine eyes are made the fools o' the other senses,
   Or else worth all the rest: I see thee still;
   And on thy blade and dudgeon[2] gouts[3] of blood,
   Which was not so before. There's no such thing:
   It is the bloody business which informs
   Thus to mine eyes. Now o'er the one half-world
   Nature seems dead, and wicked dreams abuse
   The curtain'd sleep; witchcraft celebrates
   Pale Hecate's offerings; and wither'd murder,

[2] *dudgeon*] handle.
[3] *gouts*] drops.

Alarum'd by his sentinel, the wolf,
Whose howl's his watch, thus with his stealthy pace,
With Tarquin's ravishing strides, towards his design
Moves like a ghost. Thou sure and firm-set earth,
Hear not my steps, which way they walk, for fear
Thy very stones prate of my whereabout,
And take the present horror from the time,
Which now suits with it. Whiles I threat, he lives:
Words to the heat of deeds too cold breath gives. [A *bell rings*.
I go, and it is done: the bell invites me.
Hear it not, Duncan, for it is a knell
That summons thee to heaven, or to hell.   [*Exit*.

SCENE II. *The same.*

Enter LADY MACBETH.

LADY M. That which hath made them drunk hath made me bold;
      What hath quench'd them hath given me fire. Hark! Peace!
      It was the owl that shriek'd, the fatal bellman,
      Which gives the stern'st good-night. He is about it:
      The doors are open, and the surfeited grooms[1]
      Do mock their charge with snores: I have drugg'd their pos-
         sets,[2]
      That death and nature do contend about them,
      Whether they live or die.
MACB.   [*Within*] Who's there? what, ho!
LADY M. Alack, I am afraid they have awaked
      And 'tis not done: the attempt and not the deed
      Confounds us. Hark! I laid their daggers ready;
      He could not miss 'em. Had he not resembled
      My father as he slept, I had done't.

---

[1] *grooms*] menials.
[2] *possets*] bedtime drink of hot milk curdled with ale.

Enter MACBETH.

                               My husband!

MACB.   I have done the deed. Didst thou not hear a noise?

LADY M. I heard the owl scream and the crickets cry.
         Did not you speak?

MACB.   When?

LADY M.   Now.

MACB.   As I descended?

LADY M. Ay.

MACB.   Hark!
         Who lies i' the second chamber?

LADY M.   Donalbain.

MACB.   This is a sorry sight.   [*Looking on his hands.*

LADY M. A foolish thought, to say a sorry sight.

MACB.   There's one did laugh in's sleep, and one cried 'Murder!'
         That they did wake each other: I stood and heard them:
         But they did say their prayers, and address'd them[3]
         Again to sleep.

LADY M.   There are two lodged together.

MACB.   One cried 'God bless us!' and 'Amen' the other,
         As they had seen me with these hangman's hands:
         Listening their fear, I could not say 'Amen,'
         When they did say 'God bless us!'

LADY M. Consider it not so deeply.

MACB.   But wherefore could not I pronounce 'Amen'?
         I had most need of blessing, and 'Amen'
         Stuck in my throat.

LADY M.   These deeds must not be thought
         After these ways; so, it will make us mad.

MACB.   Methought I heard a voice cry 'Sleep no more!
         Macbeth does murder sleep'—the innocent sleep,
         Sleep that knits up the ravell'd sleave[4] of care,
         The death of each day's life, sore labour's bath,
         Balm of hurt minds, great nature's second course,
         Chief nourisher in life's feast,—

---

[3] *address'd them*] made themselves ready.
[4] *sleave*] silk.

LADY M.   What do you mean?

MACB.   Still it cried 'Sleep no more!' to all the house:
         'Glamis hath murder'd sleep, and therefore Cawdor
         Shall sleep no more: Macbeth shall sleep no more.'

LADY M. Who was it that thus cried? Why, worthy thane,
         You do unbend your noble strength, to think
         So brainsickly of things. Go get some water,
         And wash this filthy witness from your hand.
         Why did you bring these daggers from the place?
         They must lie there: go carry them, and smear
         The sleepy grooms with blood.

MACB.   I'll go no more:
         I am afraid to think what I have done;
         Look on't again I dare not.

LADY M.   Infirm of purpose!
         Give me the daggers: the sleeping and the dead
         Are but as pictures: 'tis the eye of childhood
         That fears a painted devil. If he do bleed,
         I'll gild the faces of the grooms withal,
         For it must seem their guilt.   [*Exit. Knocking within.*

MACB.   Whence is that knocking?
         How is't with me, when every noise appals me?
         What hands are here? ha! they pluck out mine eyes!
         Will all great Neptune's ocean wash this blood
         Clean from my hand? No; this my hand will rather
         The multitudinous seas incarnadine,
         Making the green one red.

Re-enter LADY MACBETH.

LADY M. My hands are of your colour, but I shame
         To wear a heart so white. [*Knocking within.*] I hear a knocking
         At the south entry: retire we to our chamber:
         A little water clears us of this deed:
         How easy is it then! Your constancy
         Hath left you unattended.⁵ [*Knocking within.*] Hark! more
              knocking:
         Get on your nightgown, lest occasion call us
         And show us to be watchers: be not lost

---

⁵ *left you unattended*] abandoned you.

So poorly in your thoughts.

MACB.   To know my deed, 'twere best not know myself.

[Knocking within.

Wake Duncan with thy knocking! I would thou couldst!

[Exeunt.

SCENE III. *The same.*

Enter a Porter. *Knocking within.*

PORTER.   Here's a knocking indeed! If a man were porter of hell-gate, he
should have old¹ turning the key. [*Knocking within.*] Knock,
knock, knock! Who's there, i' the name of Beelzebub? Here's
a farmer, that hanged himself on th' expectation of plenty:²
come in time; have napkins enow about you; here you'll
sweat for't. [*Knocking within.*] Knock, knock! Who's there, in
th' other devil's name? Faith, here's an equivocator, that
could swear in both the scales against either scale; who committed treason enough for God's sake, yet could not equivocate to heaven: O, come in, equivocator. [*Knocking within.*]
Knock, knock, knock! Who's there? Faith, here's an English
tailor come hither, for stealing out of a French hose: come in,
tailor; here you may roast your goose.³ [*Knocking within.*]
Knock, knock; never at quiet! What are you? But this place is
too cold for hell. I'll devil-porter it no further: I had thought
to have let in some of all professions, that go the primrose way
to the everlasting bonfire. [*Knocking within.*] Anon, anon! I
pray you, remember the porter.   [*Opens the gate.*

Enter MACDUFF *and* LENNOX.

MACD.   Was it so late, friend, ere you went to bed,
That you do lie so late?

---

¹ *old*] too much.
² *expectation of plenty*] i.e., low prices.
³ *goose*] smoothing iron.

PORT.   Faith, sir, we were carousing till the second cock: and drink,
          sir, is a great provoker of three things.

MACD.   What three things does drink especially provoke?

PORT.   Marry, sir, nose-painting, sleep and urine. Lechery, sir, it
          provokes and unprovokes; it provokes the desire, but it takes
          away the performance: therefore much drink may be said to
          be an equivocator with lechery: it makes him and it mars
          him; it sets him on and it takes him off; it persuades him and
          disheartens him; makes him stand to and not stand to; in
          conclusion, equivocates him in a sleep, and giving him the
          lie, leaves him.

MACD.   I believe drink gave thee the lie last night.

PORT.   That it did, sir, i' the very throat on me: but I requited him for
          his lie, and, I think, being too strong for him, though he
          took up my legs sometime, yet I made a shift[4] to cast him.

MACD.   Is thy master stirring?

Enter MACBETH.

          Our knocking has awaked him; here he comes.

LEN.   Good morrow, noble sir.

MACB.   Good morrow, both.

MACD.   Is the king stirring, worthy thane?

MACB.   Not yet.

MACD.   He did command me to call timely on him:
          I have almost slipp'd the hour.

MACB.   I'll bring you to him.

MACD.   I know this is a joyful trouble to you;
          But yet 'tis one.

MACB.   The labour we delight in physics pain.
          This is the door.

MACD.   I'll make so bold to call,
          For 'tis my limited[5] service.   [*Exit.*

LEN.   Goes the king hence to-day?

MACB.   He does: he did appoint so.

LEN.   The night has been unruly: where we lay,
          Our chimneys were blown down, and, as they say,
          Lamentings heard i' the air, strange screams of death,

---

[4] *made a shift*] contrived.
[5] *limited*] appointed.

And prophesying with accents terrible
Of dire combustion and confused events
New hatch'd to the woful time: the obscure bird
Clamour'd the livelong night: some say, the earth
Was feverous and did shake.

MACB.   'Twas a rough night.
LEN.   My young remembrance cannot parallel
         A fellow to it.

Re-enter MACDUFF.

MACD.   O horror, horror, horror! Tongue nor heart
         Cannot conceive nor name thee.

MACB. ⎱
LEN. ⎰   What's the matter?

MACD.   Confusion now hath made his masterpiece.
         Most sacrilegious murder hath broke ope
         The Lord's anointed temple, and stole thence
         The life o' the building.

MACB.   What is't you say? the life?
LEN.   Mean you his majesty?
MACD.   Approach the chamber, and destroy your sight
         With a new Gorgon: do not bid me speak;
         See, and then speak yourselves. [*Exeunt Macbeth and Lennox.*
                                  Awake, awake!
         Ring the alarum-bell. Murder and treason!
         Banquo and Donalbain! Malcolm! awake!
         Shake off this downy sleep, death's counterfeit,
         And look on death itself! up, up, and see
         The great doom's image! Malcolm! Banquo!
         As from your graves rise up, and walk like sprites,
         To countenance[6] this horror. Ring the bell.   [*Bell rings.*

Enter LADY MACBETH.

LADY M. What's the business,
         That such a hideous trumpet calls to parley
         The sleepers of the house? speak, speak!
MACD.   O gentle lady,

---

[6] *countenance*] be in keeping with and behold.

'Tis not for you to hear what I can speak:
The repetition, in a woman's ear,
Would murder as it fell.

Enter BANQUO.

                              O Banquo, Banquo!
          Our royal master's murder'd.
LADY M.   Woe, alas!
          What, in our house?
BAN.   Too cruel any where.
          Dear Duff, I prithee, contradict thyself,
          And say it is not so.

Re-enter MACBETH *and* LENNOX, *with* ROSS.

MACB.   Had I but died an hour before this chance,
          I had lived a blessed time; for from this instant
          There's nothing serious in morality:[7]
          All is but toys: renown and grace is dead;
          The wine of life is drawn, and the mere lees
          Is left this vault to brag of.

Enter MALCOLM *and* DONALBAIN.

DON.   What is amiss?
MACB.   You are, and do not know't:
          The spring, the head, the fountain of your blood
          Is stopp'd; the very source of it is stopp'd.
MACD.   Your royal father's murder'd.
MAL.   O, by whom?
LEN.   Those of his chamber, as it seem'd, had done't:
          Their hands and faces were all badged with blood;
          So were their daggers, which unwiped we found
          Upon their pillows:
          They stared, and were distracted; no man's life
          Was to be trusted with them.
MACB.   O, yet I do repent me of my fury,
          That I did kill them.
MACD.   Wherefore did you so?

---

[7] *mortality*] human life.

MACB.   Who can be wise, amazed, temperate and furious,
         Loyal and neutral, in a moment? No man:
         The expedition of my violent love
         Outrun the pauser reason. Here lay Duncan,
         His silver skin laced with his golden blood,
         And his gash'd stabs look'd like a breach in nature
         For ruin's wasteful[8] entrance: there, the murderers,
         Steep'd in the colours of their trade, their daggers
         Unmannerly breech'd[9] with gore: who could refrain,
         That had a heart to love, and in that heart
         Courage to make's love known?
LADY M.   Help me hence, ho!
MACD.   Look to the lady.
MAL.   [*Aside to Don.*] Why do we hold our tongues,
         That most may claim this argument for ours?
DON.   [*Aside to Mal.*] What should be spoken here, where our fate,
         Hid in an auger-hole, may rush, and seize us?
         Let's away;
         Our tears are not yet brew'd.
MAL.   [*Aside to Don.*] Nor our strong sorrow
         Upon the foot of motion.
BAN.   Look to the lady:
                          [*Lady Macbeth is carried out.*
         And when we have our naked frailties hid,
         That suffer in exposure, let us meet,
         And question this most bloody piece of work,
         To know it further. Fears and scruples[10] shake us:
         In the great hand of God I stand, and thence
         Against the undivulged pretence[11] I fight
         Of treasonous malice.
MACD.   And so do I.
ALL.   So all.
MACB.   Let's briefly put on manly readiness,
         And meet i' the hall together.

---

[8] *wasteful*] destructive.
[9] *breech'd*] sheathed, covered.
[10] *scruples*] doubts.
[11] *pretence*] purpose, design.

ALL.   Well contented.

                    [*Exeunt all but Malcolm and Donalbain.*

MAL.   What will you do? Let's not consort with them:
            To show an unfelt sorrow is an office
            Which the false man does easy. I'll to England.
DON.   To Ireland, I; our separated fortune
            Shall keep us both the safer: where we are
            There's daggers in men's smiles: the near in blood,
            The nearer bloody.
MAL.   This murderous shaft that's shot
            Hath not yet lighted, and our safest way
            Is to avoid the aim. Therefore to horse;
            And let us not be dainty of leave-taking,
            But shift away:[12] there's warrant in that theft
            Which steals itself when there's no mercy left.   [*Exeunt.*

SCENE IV. *Outside Macbeth's castle.*

Enter ROSS *with an* old Man.

OLD M.   Threescore and ten I can remember well:
            Within the volume of which time I have seen
            Hours dreadful and things strange, but this sore night
            Hath trifled former knowings.
ROSS.   Ah, good father,
            Thou seest, the heavens, as troubled with man's act,
            Threaten his bloody stage: by the clock 'tis day,
            And yet dark night strangles the travelling lamp:
            Is't night's predominance, or the day's shame,
            That darkness does the face of earth entomb,
            When living light should kiss it?
OLD M.   'Tis unnatural,

---

[12] *shift away*] contrive to get away.

Even like the deed that's done. On Tuesday last
A falcon towering in her pride of place
Was by a mousing owl hawk'd at and kill'd.

ROSS. And Duncan's horses—a thing most strange and certain—
Beauteous and swift, the minions[1] of their race,
Turn'd wild in nature, broke their stalls, flung out,
Contending 'gainst obedience, as they would make
War with mankind.

OLD M.   'Tis said they eat each other.

ROSS. They did so, to the amazement of mine eyes,
That look'd upon't.

Enter MACDUFF.

            Here comes the good Macduff.
How goes the world, sir, now?

MACD.   Why, see you not?

ROSS. Is't known who did this more than bloody deed?

MACD. Those that Macbeth hath slain.

ROSS.   Alas, the day!
What good could they pretend?[2]

MACD.   They were suborn'd:
Malcolm and Donalbain, the king's two sons,
Are stol'n away and fled, which puts upon them
Suspicion of the deed.

ROSS.   'Gainst nature still:
Thriftless ambition, that wilt ravin up
Thine own life's means! Then 'tis most like
The sovereignty will fall upon Macbeth.

MACD. He is already named, and gone to Scone
To be invested.

ROSS.   Where is Duncan's body?

MACD. Carried to Colme-kill,
The sacred storehouse of his predecessors
And guardian of their bones.

ROSS.   Will you to Scone?

MACD. No, cousin, I'll to Fife.

---

[1] *minions*] darlings, favorites.
[2] *pretend*] intend.

ROSS.   Well, I will thither.

MACD.   Well, may you see things well done there: adieu!
          Lest our old robes sit easier than our new!

ROSS.   Farewell, father.

OLD M.   God's benison go with you, and with those
          That would make good of bad and friends of foes! [*Exeunt.*

ACT III.

SCENE I. *Forres. The palace.*

Enter BANQUO.

BAN.   Thou hast it now: king, Cawdor, Glamis, all,
As the weird women promised, and I fear
Thou play'dst most foully for't: yet it was said
It should not stand in thy posterity,
But that myself should be the root and father
Of many kings. If there come truth from them—
As upon thee, Macbeth, their speeches shine—
Why, by the verities on thee made good,
May they not be my oracles as well
And set me up in hope? But hush, no more.

Sennet sounded. Enter MACBETH, *as king;* LADY MACBETH, *as queen;*
LENNOX, ROSS, Lords, Ladies, *and* Attendants.

MACB.   Here's our chief guest.
LADY M.   If he had been forgotten,
It had been as a gap in our great feast,
And all-thing[1] unbecoming.
MACB.   To-night we hold a solemn[2] supper, sir,
And I'll request your presence.
BAN.   Let your highness
Command upon me, to the which my duties
Are with a most indissoluble tie
For ever knit.
MACB.   Ride you this afternoon?
BAN.   Ay, my good lord.

[1] *all-thing*] altogether.
[2] *solemn*] formal.

33

MACB.   We should have else desired your good advice,
          Which still[3] hath been both grave and prosperous,
          In this day's council; but we'll take to-morrow.
          Is't far you ride?

BAN.   As far, my lord, as will fill up the time
          'Twixt this and supper: go not my horse the better,
          I must become a borrower of the night
          For a dark hour or twain.

MACB.   Fail not our feast.

BAN.   My lord, I will not.

MACB.   We hear our bloody cousins are bestow'd
          In England and in Ireland, not confessing
          Their cruel parricide, filling their hearers
          With strange invention: but of that to-morrow,
          When therewithal we shall have cause[4] of state
          Craving us jointly. Hie you to horse: adieu,
          Till you return at night. Goes Fleance with you?

BAN.   Ay, my good lord: our time does call upon's.

MACB.   I wish your horses swift and sure of foot,
          And so I do commend you to their backs.
          Farewell.   *[Exit Banquo.*
          Let every man be master of his time
          Till seven at night; to make society
          The sweeter welcome, we will keep ourself
          Till supper-time alone: while[5] then, God be with you!

                [Exeunt all but Macbeth and an Attendant.

          Sirrah, a word with you: attend those men
          Our pleasure?

ATTEND.   They are, my lord, without the palace-gate.

MACB.   Bring them before us.   *[Exit Attendant.*
                    To be thus is nothing;
          But to be safely thus: our fears in Banquo
          Stick deep; and in his royalty of nature

[3] *still*] always.
[4] *cause*] affairs.
[5] *while*] until.

Reigns that which would be fear'd: 'tis much he dares,
And, to that dauntless temper of his mind,
He hath a wisdom that doth guide his valour
To act in safety. There is none but he
Whose being I do fear: and under him
My Genius is rebuked, as it is said
Mark Antony's was by Cæsar. He chid the sisters,
When first they put the name of king upon me,
And bade them speak to him; then prophet-like
They hail'd him father to a line of kings:
Upon my head they placed a fruitless crown
And put a barren sceptre in my gripe,
Thence to be wrench'd with an unlineal hand,
No son of mine succeeding. If't be so,
For Banquo's issue have I filed[6] my mind;
For them the gracious Duncan have I murder'd;
Put rancours in the vessel of my peace
Only for them, and mine eternal jewel
Given to the common enemy of man,
To make them kings, the seed of Banquo kings!
Rather than so, come, fate, into the list,
And champion me to the utterance![7] Who's there?

Re-enter Attendant, *with two* Murderers.

Now go to the door, and stay there till we call. [*Exit Attendant.*
Was it not yesterday we spoke together?
FIRST MUR.   It was, so please your highness.
MACB.   Well then, now
Have you consider'd of my speeches? Know
That it was he in the times past which held you
So under fortune, which you thought had been
Our innocent self: this I made good to you
In our last conference; pass'd in probation with you,
How you were borne in hand,[8] how cross'd, the instruments,
Who wrought with them, and all things else that might

---

[6] *filed*] defiled.
[7] *utterance*] uttermost.
[8] *borne in hand*] tricked.

> To half a soul and to a notion[9] crazed
> Say 'Thus did Banquo.'

FIRST MUR.   You made it known to us.

MACB.   I did so; and went further, which is now
>   Our point of second meeting. Do you find
>   Your patience so predominant in your nature,
>   That you can let this go? Are you so gospell'd,[10]
>   To pray for this good man and for his issue,
>   Whose heavy hand hath bow'd you to the grave
>   And beggar'd yours for ever?

FIRST MUR.   We are men, my liege.

MACB.   Ay, in the catalogue ye go for men;
>   As hounds and greyhounds, mongrels, spaniels, curs,
>   Shoughs, water-rugs[11] and demi-wolves, are clept[12]
>   All by the name of dogs: the valued file
>   Distinguishes the swift, the slow, the subtle,
>   The housekeeper, the hunter, every one
>   According to the gift which bounteous nature
>   Hath in him closed, whereby he does receive
>   Particular addition, from the bill
>   That writes them all alike: and so of men.
>   Now if you have a station in the file,
>   Not i' the worst rank of manhood, say it,
>   And I will put that business in your bosoms
>   Whose execution takes your enemy off,
>   Grapples you to the heart and love of us,
>   Who wear our health but sickly in his life,
>   Which in his death were perfect.

SEC. MUR.   I am one, my liege,
>   Whom the vile blows and buffets of the world
>   Have so incensed that I am reckless what
>   I do to spite the world.

FIRST MUR.   And I another
>   So weary with disasters, tugg'd with fortune,
>   That I would set my life on any chance,

---

[9] *notion*] mind.

[10] *gospell'd*] inclined to act according to the precepts of the Gospels.

[11] *Shoughs, water-rugs*] shaggy dogs, poodles.

[12] *clept*] called.

To mend it or be rid on 't.

MACB.   Both of you
Know Banquo was your enemy.

BOTH MUR.   True, my lord.

MACB.   So is he mine, and in such bloody distance
That every minute of his being thrusts
Against my near'st of life: and though I could
With barefaced power sweep him from my sight
And bid my will avouch it, yet I must not,
For certain friends that are both his and mine,
Whose loves I may not drop, but wail his fall
Who I myself struck down: and thence it is
That I to your assistance do make love,
Masking the business from the common eye
For sundry weighty reasons.

SEC. MUR.   We shall, my lord,
Perform what you command us.

FIRST MUR.   Though our lives—

MACB.   Your spirits shine through you. Within this hour at most
I will advise you where to plant yourselves,
Acquaint you with the perfect spy o' the time,
The moment on 't; for 't must be done to-night,
And something[13] from the palace; always thought
That I require a clearness:[14] and with him—
To leave no rubs nor botches in the work—
Fleance his son, that keeps him company,
Whose absence is no less material to me
Than is his father's, must embrace the fate
Of that dark hour. Resolve yourselves apart:
I'll come to you anon.

BOTH MUR.   We are resolved, my lord.

MACB.   I'll call upon you straight: abide within. [*Exeunt Murderers.*
It is concluded: Banquo, thy soul's flight,
If it find heaven, must find it out to-night.   [*Exit.*

---

[13] *something*] somewhat.
[14] *clearness*] i.e., alibi.

SCENE II. *The palace.*

Enter LADY MACBETH *and a* Servant.

LADY M. Is Banquo gone from court?
SERV. Ay, madam, but returns again to-night.
LADY M. Say to the king, I would attend his leisure
  For a few words.
SERV.   Madam, I will.   [*Exit.*
LADY M.   Nought's had, all's spent,
  Where our desire is got without content:
  'Tis safer to be that which we destroy
  Than by destruction dwell in doubtful joy.

Enter MACBETH.

  How now, my lord! why do you keep alone,
  Of sorriest fancies your companions making;
  Using those thoughts which should indeed have died
  With them they think on? Things without all remedy
  Should be without regard: what's done is done.
MACB. We have scotch'd[1] the snake, not kill'd it:
  She'll close and be herself, whilst our poor malice
  Remains in danger of her former tooth.
  But let the frame of things disjoint, both the worlds suffer,
  Ere we will eat our meal in fear, and sleep
  In the affliction of these terrible dreams
  That shake us nightly: better be with the dead,
  Whom we, to gain our peace, have sent to peace,
  Than on the torture of the mind to lie
  In restless ecstasy.[2] Duncan is in his grave;
  After life's fitful fever he sleeps well;
  Treason has done his worst: nor steel, nor poison,
  Malice domestic, foreign levy, nothing,
  Can touch him further.

---

[1] *scotch'd*] slashed.
[2] *ecstasy*] mental alienation.

LADY M.   Come on;
                  Gentle my lord, sleek o'er your rugged looks;
                  Be bright and jovial among your guests to-night.
MACB.   So shall I, love; and so, I pray, be you:
                  Let your remembrance apply to Banquo;
                  Present him eminence, both with eye and tongue:
                  Unsafe the while, that we
                  Must lave our honours in these flattering streams,
                  And make our faces visards to our hearts,
                  Disguising what they are.
LADY M.   You must leave this.
MACB.   O, full of scorpions is my mind, dear wife!
                  Thou know'st that Banquo, and his Fleance, lives.
LADY M. But in them nature's copy's not eterne.
MACB.   There's comfort yet; they are assailable;
                  Then be thou jocund: ere the bat hath flown
                  His cloister'd flight; ere to black Hecate's summons
                  The shard-borne³ beetle with his drowsy hums
                  Hath rung night's yawning peal, there shall be done
                  A deed of dreadful note.
LADY M.   What's to be done?
MACB.   Be innocent of the knowledge, dearest chuck,
                  Till thou applaud the deed. Come, seeling⁴ night,
                  Scarf up the tender eye of pitiful day,
                  And with thy bloody and invisible hand
                  Cancel and tear to pieces that great bond
                  Which keeps me pale! Light thickens, and the crow
                  Makes wing to the rooky wood:
                  Good things of day begin to droop and drowse,
                  Whiles night's black agents to their preys do rouse.
                  Thou marvell'st at my words: but hold thee still;
                  Things bad begun make strong themselves by ill:
                  So, prithee, go with me.   [*Exeunt.*

---

³ *shard-borne*] borne on scaly wings.
⁴ *seeling*] blinding. The term, from falconry, refers to the sewing together of the bird's eyelids.

SCENE III. *A park near the palace.*

Enter three Murderers.

FIRST MUR.   But who did bid thee join with us?
THIRD MUR.   Macbeth.
SEC. MUR.   He needs not our mistrust; since he delivers
    Our offices, and what we have to do,
    To the direction just.[1]
FIRST MUR.   Then stand with us.
    The west yet glimmers with some streaks of day:
    Now spurs the lated[2] traveller apace
    To gain the timely inn, and near approaches
    The subject of our watch.
THIRD MUR.   Hark! I hear horses.
BAN.   [*Within*] Give us a light there, ho!
SEC. MUR.   Then 'tis he: the rest
    That are within the note of expectation[3]
    Already are i' the court.
FIRST MUR.   His horses go about.
THIRD MUR.   Almost a mile: but he does usually—
    So all men do—from hence to the palace gate
    Make it their walk.
SEC. MUR.   A light, a light!

Enter BANQUO, *and* FLEANCE *with a torch.*

THIRD MUR.   'Tis he.
FIRST MUR.   Stand to 't.
BAN.   It will be rain to-night.
FIRST MUR.   Let it come down.
                   [*They set upon Banquo.*
BAN.   O, treachery! Fly, good Fleance, fly, fly, fly!
    Thou mayst revenge. O slave!   [*Dies. Fleance escapes.*
THIRD MUR.   Who did strike out the light?
FIRST MUR.   Was't not the way?

[1] *To the direction just*] according to Macbeth's instructions.
[2] *lated*] belated.
[3] *note of expectation*] list of those expected.

THIRD MUR.   There's but one down; the son is fled.
SEC. MUR.   We have lost
          Best half of our affair.
FIRST MUR.   Well, let's away and say how much is done.   [*Exeunt.*

SCENE IV. *Hall in the palace.*

A banquet prepared. Enter MACBETH, LADY MACBETH, ROSS, LENNOX,
Lords, *and* Attendants.

MACB.   You know your own degrees; sit down: at first
          And last the hearty welcome.
LORDS.   Thanks to your majesty.
MACB.   Ourself will mingle with society
          And play the humble host.
          Our hostess keeps her state,[1] but in best time
          We will require[2] her welcome.
LADY M.   Pronounce it for me, sir, to all our friends,
          For my heart speaks they are welcome.

Enter first Murderer *to the door.*

MACB.   See, they encounter thee with their hearts' thanks.
          Both sides are even: here I'll sit i' the midst:
          Be large[3] in mirth; anon we'll drink a measure
          The table round. [*Approaching the door*] There's blood upon
              thy face.
MUR.   'Tis Banquo's then.
MACB.   'Tis better thee without than he within.
          Is he dispatch'd?
MUR.   My lord, his throat is cut; that I did for him.
MACB.   Thou art the best o' the cut-throats: yet he's good
          That did the like for Fleance: if thou didst it,

[1] *state*] canopied chair of state.
[2] *require*] request.
[3] *large*] liberal.

	Thou art the nonpareil.[4]
MUR.	Most royal sir,

Fleance is 'scaped.

MACB.   [*Aside*] Then comes my fit again: I had else been perfect,
Whole as the marble, founded as the rock,
As broad and general as the casing air:[5]
But now I am cabin'd, cribb'd,[6] confined, bound in
To saucy[7] doubts and fears.—But Banquo's safe?

MUR.   Ay, my good lord: safe in a ditch he bides,
With twenty trenched[8] gashes on his head;
The least a death to nature.

MACB.   Thanks for that.
[*Aside*] There the grown serpent lies; the worm[9] that's fled
Hath nature that in time will venom breed,
No teeth for the present. Get thee gone: to-morrow
We'll hear ourselves again.[10]   [*Exit Murderer.*

LADY M.   My royal lord,
You do not give the cheer: the feast is sold
That is not often vouch'd,[11] while 'tis a-making,
'Tis given with welcome: to feed were best at home;
From thence[12] the sauce to meat is ceremony;
Meeting were bare without it.

MACB.   Sweet remembrancer!
Now good digestion wait on appetite,
And health on both!

LEN.   May't please your highness sit.

[*The Ghost of Banquo enters, and sits in Macbeth's place.*

MACB.   Here had we now our country's honour roof'd,
Were the graced[13] person of our Banquo present;

---

[4] *nonpareil*] paragon.
[5] *broad . . . air*] free and unrestrained as the surrounding air.
[6] *cribb'd*] caged.
[7] *saucy*] unbounded.
[8] *trenched*] cut.
[9] *worm*] serpent.
[10] *hear ourselves again*] discuss things further.
[11] *vouch'd*] asserted.
[12] *From thence*] away from home.
[13] *graced*] dignified.

	Who may I rather challenge for unkindness
	Than pity for mischance!
Ross.	His absence, sir,
	Lays blame upon his promise. Please't your highness
	To grace us with your royal company.
Macb.	The table's full.
Len.	Here is a place reserved, sir.
Macb.	Where?
Len.	Here, my good lord. What is't that moves your highness?
Macb.	Which of you have done this?
Lords.	What, my good lord?
Macb.	Thou canst not say I did it: never shake
	Thy gory locks at me.
Ross.	Gentlemen, rise; his highness is not well.
Lady M.	Sit, worthy friends: my lord is often thus,
	And hath been from his youth: pray you, keep seat;
	The fit is momentary; upon a thought[14]
	He will again be well: if much you note him,
	You shall offend him and extend his passion:
	Feed, and regard him not. Are you a man?
Macb.	Ay, and a bold one, that dare look on that
	Which might appal the devil.
Lady M.	O proper stuff!
	This is the very painting of your fear:
	This is the air-drawn dagger which, you said,
	Led you to Duncan. O, these flaws[15] and starts,
	Impostors to true fear, would well become
	A woman's story at a winter's fire,
	Authorized by her grandam. Shame itself!
	Why do you make such faces? When all's done,
	You look but on a stool.
Macb.	Prithee, see there! behold! look! lo! how say you?
	Why, what care I? If thou canst nod, speak too.
	If charnel-houses and our graves must send
	Those that we bury back, our monuments
	Shall be the maws of kites. [*Exit Ghost.*

---

[14] *upon a thought*] in no time.
[15] *flaws*] storms of passion.

LADY M.   What, quite unmann'd in folly?
MACB.   If I stand here, I saw him.
LADY M.   Fie, for shame!
MACB.   Blood hath been shed ere now, i' the olden time,
         Ere humane statute purged the gentle weal;
         Ay, and since too, murders have been perform'd
         Too terrible for the ear: the time has been,
         That, when the brains were out, the man would die,
         And there an end; but now they rise again,
         With twenty mortal murders[16] on their crowns,
         And push us from our stools: this is more strange
         Than such a murder is.
LADY M.   My worthy lord,
         Your noble friends do lack you.
MACB.   I do forget.
         Do not muse at me, my most worthy friends;
         I have a strange infirmity, which is nothing
         To those that know me. Come, love and health to all;
         Then I'll sit down. Give me some wine, fill full.
         I drink to the general joy o' the whole table,
         And to our dear friend Banquo, whom we miss;
         Would he were here! to all and him we thirst,
         And all to all.
LORDS.   Our duties, and the pledge.

Re-enter Ghost.

MACB.   Avaunt! and quit my sight! let the earth hide thee!
         Thy bones are marrowless, thy blood is cold;
         Thou hast no speculation[17] in those eyes
         Which thou dost glare with.
LADY M.   Think of this, good peers,
         But as a thing of custom: 'tis no other;
         Only it spoils the pleasure of the time.
MACB.   What man dare, I dare:
         Approach thou like the rugged Russian bear,
         The arm'd rhinoceros, or the Hyrcan tiger;

---

[16] *mortal murders*] fatal wounds.
[17] *speculation*] power of intelligent vision.

Take any shape but that, and my firm nerves
Shall never tremble: or be alive again,
And dare me to the desert with thy sword;
If trembling I inhabit then, protest me
The baby of a girl. Hence, horrible shadow!
Unreal mockery, hence!   [*Exit Ghost.*
     Why, so: being gone,
I am a man again. Pray you, sit still.

LADY M. You have displaced the mirth, broke the good meeting,
With most admired disorder.[18]

MACB.   Can such things be,
And overcome[19] us like a summer's cloud,
Without our special wonder? You make me strange
Even to the disposition that I owe,[20]
When now I think you can behold such sights,
And keep the natural ruby of your cheeks,
When mine is blanch'd with fear.

ROSS.   What sights, my lord?

LADY M. I pray you, speak not; he grows worse and worse;
Question enrages him: at once, good night:
Stand not upon the order of your going,
But go at once.

LEN.   Good night; and better health
Attend his majesty!

LADY M.   A kind good night to all!

    [*Exeunt all but Macbeth and Lady M.*

MACB. It will have blood: they say blood will have blood:
Stones have been known to move and trees to speak;
Augures[21] and understood relations have
By maggot-pies[22] and choughs and rooks brought forth
The secret'st man of blood. What is the night?

LADY M. Almost at odds with morning, which is which.

MACB. How say'st thou, that Macduff denies his person

---

[18] *admired disorder*] amazing mental derangement.
[19] *overcome*] pass over.
[20] *owe*] possess.
[21] *Augures*] auguries.
[22] *maggot-pies*] magpies.

	At our great bidding?
LADY M.	Did you send to him, sir?
MACB.	I hear it by the way, but I will send:

There's not a one of them but in his house
I keep a servant fee'd. I will to-morrow,
And betimes I will, to the weird sisters:
More shall they speak, for now I am bent to know,
By the worst means, the worst. For mine own good
All causes shall give way: I am in blood
Stepp'd in so far that, should I wade no more,
Returning were as tedious as go o'er:
Strange things I have in head that will to hand,
Which must be acted ere they may be scann'd.

LADY M. You lack the season of all natures, sleep.

MACB.   Come, we'll to sleep. My strange and self-abuse[23]
Is the initiate fear[24] that wants hard use:
We are yet but young in deed.   [*Exeunt.*

SCENE V. *A heath.*

Thunder. Enter the three Witches, *meeting* HECATE.

FIRST WITCH.   Why, how now, Hecate! you look angerly.

HEC.   Have I not reason, beldams as you are,
        Saucy and over-bold? How did you dare
        To trade and traffic with Macbeth
        In riddles and affairs of death;
        And I, the mistress of your charms,
        The close contriver of all harms,
        Was never call'd to bear my part,
        Or show the glory of our art?
        And, which is worse, all you have done
        Hath been but for a wayward son,
        Spiteful and wrathful; who, as others do,

---

[23] *self-abuse*] delusion.
[24] *initiate fear*] novice's fear.

Loves for his own ends, not for you.
But make amends now: get you gone,
And at the pit of Acheron
Meet me i' the morning: thither he
Will come to know his destiny:
Your vessels and your spells provide,
Your charms and every thing beside.
I am for the air; this night I'll spend
Unto a dismal[1] and a fatal end:
Great business must be wrought ere noon:
Upon the corner of the moon
There hangs a vaporous drop profound;
I'll catch it ere it come to ground:
And that distill'd by magic sleights
Shall raise such artificial[2] sprites
As by the strength of their illusion
Shall draw him on to his confusion:
He shall spurn fate, scorn death, and bear
His hopes 'bove wisdom, grace and fear:
And you all know security[3]
Is mortals' chiefest enemy.

        [*Music and a song within:* 'Come away, come away,' &c.

Hark! I am call'd; my little spirit, see,
Sits in a foggy cloud, and stays for me.   [*Exit.*
FIRST WITCH.   Come, let's make haste; she'll soon be back again.
                                          [*Exeunt.*

SCENE VI. *Forres. The palace.*

Enter LENNOX *and another* Lord.

LEN.   My former speeches have but hit your thoughts,
         Which can interpret farther: only I say

[1] *dismal*] disastrous.
[2] *artificial*] artful, cunning.
[3] *security*] overconfidence, carelessness.

Things have been strangely borne.[1] The gracious Duncan
Was pitied of Macbeth: marry, he was dead:
And the right-valiant Banquo walk'd too late;
Whom, you may say, if't please you, Fleance kill'd,
For Fleance fled: men must not walk too late.
Who cannot want the thought, how monstrous
It was for Malcolm and for Donalbain
To kill their gracious father? damned fact![2]
How it did grieve Macbeth! did he not straight,
In pious rage, the two delinquents tear,
That were the slaves of drink and thralls of sleep?
Was not that nobly done? Ay, and wisely too;
For 'twould have anger'd any heart alive
To hear the men deny't. So that, I say,
He has borne all things well: and I do think
That, had he Duncan's sons under his key—
As, an't please heaven, he shall not—they should find
What 'twere to kill a father; so should Fleance.
But, peace! for from broad words, and 'cause he fail'd
His presence at the tyrant's feast, I hear,
Macduff lives in disgrace: sir, can you tell
Where he bestows himself?

LORD.   The son of Duncan,
From whom this tyrant holds the due of birth,
Lives in the English court, and is received
Of the most pious Edward with such grace
That the malevolence of fortune nothing
Takes from his high respect. Thither Macduff
Is gone to pray the holy king, upon his aid
To wake Northumberland and warlike Siward:
That by the help of these, with Him above
To ratify the work, we may again
Give to our tables meat, sleep to our nights,
Free from our feasts and banquets bloody knives,
Do faithful homage and receive free honours:
All which we pine for now: and this report

---

[1] *borne*] conducted.
[2] *fact*] deed.

        Hath so exasperate the king that he
        Prepares for some attempt of war.
LEN.   Sent he to Macduff?
LORD.   He did: and with an absolute 'Sir, not I,'
        The cloudy[3] messenger turns me his back,
        And hums, as who should say 'You'll rue the time
        That clogs me with this answer.'
LEN.   And that well might
        Advise him to a caution, to hold what distance
        His wisdom can provide. Some holy angel
        Fly to the court of England and unfold
        His message ere he come, that a swift blessing
        May soon return to this our suffering country
        Under a hand accursed!
LORD.   I'll send my prayers with him.
                                  [Exeunt.

---

[3] *cloudy*] morose.

ACT IV.

SCENE I. *A cavern. In the middle, a boiling cauldron.*

Thunder. Enter the three Witches.

FIRST WITCH.   Thrice the brinded[1] cat hath mew'd.
SEC. WITCH.   Thrice and once the hedge-pig[2] whined.
THIRD WITCH.   Harpier cries ' 'Tis time, 'tis time.'
FIRST WITCH.   Round about the cauldron go:
        In the poison'd entrails throw.
        Toad, that under cold stone
        Days and nights has thirty one
        Swelter'd[3] venom sleeping got,
        Boil thou first i' the charmed pot.
ALL.   Double, double toil and trouble;
        Fire burn and cauldron bubble.
SEC. WITCH.   Fillet of a fenny snake,
        In the cauldron boil and bake;
        Eye of newt and toe of frog,
        Wool of bat and tongue of dog,
        Adder's fork[4] and blind-worm's sting,
        Lizard's leg and howlet's wing,
        For a charm of powerful trouble,
        Like a hell-broth boil and bubble.
ALL.   Double, double toil and trouble;
        Fire burn and cauldron bubble.
THIRD WITCH.   Scale of dragon, tooth of wolf,

---

[1] *brinded*] spotted, brindled.
[2] *hedge-pig*] hedgehog.
[3] *Swelter'd*] exuded.
[4] *fork*] forked tongue.

Witches' mummy, maw and gulf[5]
Of the ravin'd salt-sea shark,
Root of hemlock digg'd i' the dark,
Liver of blaspheming Jew,
Gall of goat and slips of yew
Sliver'd[6] in the moon's eclipse,
Nose of Turk and Tartar's lips,
Finger of birth-strangled babe
Ditch-deliver'd by a drab,
Make the gruel thick and slab:[7]
Add thereto a tiger's chaudron,[8]
For the ingredients of our cauldron.

ALL.   Double, double toil and trouble;
              Fire burn and cauldron bubble.

SEC. WITCH.   Cool it with a baboon's blood,
               Then the charm is firm and good.

Enter HECATE *to the other three* Witches.

HEC.   O, well done! I commend your pains;
              And every one shall share i' the gains:
              And now about the cauldron sing,
              Like elves and fairies in a ring,
              Enchanting all that you put in.

                              [*Music and a song:* 'Black spirits,' &c.
                              [*Hecate retires.*

SEC. WITCH.   By the pricking of my thumbs,
               Something wicked this way comes:
               Open, locks,
               Whoever knocks!

Enter MACBETH.

MACB.   How now, you secret, black, and midnight hags!
              What is't you do?
ALL.   A deed without a name.

---

[5] *gulf*] gullet.
[6] *Sliver'd*] broken off.
[7] *slab*] glutinous.
[8] *chaudron*] entrails.

MACB.   I conjure you, by that which you profess,
        Howe'er you come to know it, answer me:
        Though you untie the winds and let them fight
        Against the churches; though the yesty⁹ waves
        Confound and swallow navigation up;
        Though bladed corn be lodged¹⁰ and trees blown down;
        Though castles topple on their warders' heads;
        Though palaces and pyramids do slope
        Their heads to their foundations; though the treasure
        Of nature's germens¹¹ tumble all together,
        Even till destruction sicken; answer me
        To what I ask you.
FIRST WITCH.   Speak.
SEC. WITCH.   Demand.
THIRD WITCH.   We'll answer.
FIRST WITCH.   Say, if thou'dst rather hear it from our mouths,
        Or from our masters?
MACB.   Call 'em, let me see 'em.
FIRST WITCH.   Pour in sow's blood, that hath eaten
        Her nine farrow;¹² grease that's sweaten
        From the murderer's gibbet throw
        Into the flame.
ALL.   Come, high or low;
        Thyself and office deftly show!

Thunder. First Apparition: *an armed Head.*

MACB.   Tell me, thou unknown power,—
FIRST WITCH.   He knows thy thought:
        Hear his speech, but say thou nought.
FIRST APP.   Macbeth! Macbeth! Macbeth! beware Macduff;
        Beware the thane of Fife. Dismiss me: enough. [*Descends.*
MACB.   Whate'er thou art, for thy good caution thanks;
        Thou hast harp'd¹³ my fear aright: but one word more,—
FIRST WITCH.   He will not be commanded: here's another,

---

⁹ *yesty*] foamy.
¹⁰ *lodged*] beaten flat.
¹¹ *germens*] seeds.
¹² *farrow*] litter.
¹³ *harp'd*] hit upon.

More potent than the first.

Thunder. Second Apparition: *a bloody Child.*

SEC. APP.   Macbeth! Macbeth! Macbeth!
MACB.   Had I three ears, I'd hear thee.
SEC. APP.   Be bloody, bold and resolute; laugh to scorn
                  The power of man, for none of woman born
                  Shall harm Macbeth.   [*Descends.*
MACB.   Then live, Macduff: what need I fear of thee?
                  But yet I'll make assurance double sure,
                  And take a bond of fate: thou shalt not live;
                  That I may tell pale-hearted fear it lies,
                  And sleep in spite of thunder.

Thunder. Third Apparition: *a Child crowned, with a tree in his hand.*

                                                 What is this,
                  That rises like the issue of a king,
                  And wears upon his baby-brow the round
                  And top of sovereignty?
ALL.   Listen, but speak not to't.
THIRD APP.   Be lion-mettled, proud, and take no care
                  Who chafes, who frets, or where conspirers are:
                  Macbeth shall never vanquish'd be until
                  Great Birnam wood to high Dunsinane hill
                  Shall come against him.   [*Descends.*

MACB.   That will never be:
                  Who can impress the forest, bid the tree
                  Unfix his earth-bound root? Sweet bodements! good!
                  Rebellion's head, rise never, till the wood
                  Of Birnam rise, and our high-placed Macbeth
                  Shall live the lease of nature, pay his breath
                  To time and mortal custom. Yet my heart
                  Throbs to know one thing: tell me, if your art
                  Can tell so much: shall Banquo's issue ever
                  Reign in this kingdom?
ALL.   Seek to know no more.
MACB.   I will be satisfied: deny me this,
                  And an eternal curse fall on you! Let me know:

Why sinks that cauldron? and what noise[14] is this? [*Hautboys.*
FIRST WITCH.   Show!
SEC. WITCH.   Show!
THIRD WITCH.   Show!
ALL.   Show his eyes, and grieve his heart;
    Come like shadows, so depart!

A show of eight Kings, *the last with a glass in his hand; Banquo's Ghost following.*

MACB.   Thou art too like the spirit of Banquo: down!
    Thy crown does sear mine eye-balls. And thy hair,
    Thou other gold-bound brow, is like the first.
    A third is like the former. Filthy hags!
    Why do you show me this? A fourth! Start, eyes!
    What, will the line stretch out to the crack of doom?
    Another yet! A seventh! I'll see no more:
    And yet the eighth appears, who bears a glass
    Which shows me many more; and some I see
    That two-fold balls and treble sceptres carry:
    Horrible sight! Now I see 'tis true;
    For the blood-bolter'd[15] Banquo smiles upon me,
    And points at them for his. What, is this so?
FIRST WITCH.   Ay, sir, all this is so: but why
    Stands Macbeth thus amazedly?
    Come, sisters, cheer we up his sprites,
    And show the best of our delights:
    I'll charm the air to give a sound,
    While you perform your antic round,[16]
    That this great king may kindly say
    Our duties did his welcome pay.

     [*Music. The Witches dance, and then vanish, with Hecate.*

MACB.   Where are they? Gone? Let this pernicious hour
    Stand aye accursed in the calendar!
    Come in, without there!

---

[14] *noise*] music.
[15] *blood-bolter'd*] with blood-clotted hair.
[16] *antic round*] old and fantastic dance.

Enter LENNOX.

LEN.	What's your grace's will?
MACB.	Saw you the weird sisters?
LEN.	No, my lord.
MACB.	Came they not by you?
LEN.	No indeed, my lord.

MACB.   Infected be the air whereon they ride,
And damn'd all those that trust them! I did hear
The galloping of horse: who was't came by?

LEN.   'Tis two or three, my lord, that bring you word
Macduff is fled to England.

MACB.   Fled to England!

LEN.   Ay, my good lord.

MACB.   [*Aside*] Time, thou anticipatest my dread exploits:
The flighty purpose never is o'ertook
Unless the deed go with it: from this moment
The very firstlings of my heart shall be
The firstlings of my hand. And even now,
To crown my thoughts with acts, be it thought and done:
The castle of Macduff I will surprise;
Seize upon Fife; give to the edge o' the sword
His wife, his babes, and all unfortunate souls
That trace him in his line. No boasting like a fool;
This deed I'll do before this purpose cool:
But no more sights!—Where are these gentlemen?
Come, bring me where they are.   [*Exeunt*.

SCENE II. *Fife. Macduff's castle.*

Enter LADY MACDUFF, *her* SON, *and* ROSS.

L. MACD.   What had he done, to make him fly the land?

ROSS.   You must have patience, madam.

L. MACD.   He had none:
His flight was madness: when our actions do not,
Our fears do make us traitors.

ROSS.   You know not
          Whether it was his wisdom or his fear.
L. MACD.   Wisdom! to leave his wife, to leave his babes,
          His mansion and his titles,[1] in a place
          From whence himself does fly? He loves us not;
          He wants the natural touch:[2] for the poor wren,
          The most diminutive of birds, will fight,
          Her young ones in her nest, against the owl.
          All is the fear and nothing is the love;
          As little is the wisdom, where the flight
          So runs against all reason.
ROSS.   My dearest coz,
          I pray you, school[3] yourself: but, for your husband,
          He is noble, wise, judicious, and best knows
          The fits o' the season. I dare not speak much further:
          But cruel are the times, when we are traitors
          And do not know ourselves; when we hold rumour
          From what we fear, yet know not what we fear,
          But float upon a wild and violent sea
          Each way and move. I take my leave of you:
          Shall not be long but I'll be here again:
          Things at the worst will cease, or else climb upward
          To what they were before. My pretty cousin,
          Blessing upon you!
L. MACD.   Father'd he is, and yet he's fatherless.
ROSS.   I am so much a fool, should I stay longer,
          It would be my disgrace and your discomfort:
          I take my leave at once.   [*Exit.*

L. MACD.   Sirrah, your father's dead:
          And what will you do now? How will you live?
SON.   As birds do, mother.
L. MACD.   What, with worms and flies?
SON.   With what I get, I mean; and so do they.
L. MACD.   Poor bird! thou'ldst never fear the net nor lime,
          The pitfall nor the gin.
SON.   Why should I, mother? Poor birds they are not set for.

---

   [1] *titles*] possessions.
   [2] *touch*] feeling, affection.
   [3] *school*] control.

My father is not dead, for all your saying.

L. MACD.   Yes, he is dead: how wilt thou do for a father?

SON.   Nay, how will you do for a husband?

L. MACD.   Why, I can buy me twenty at any market.

SON.   Then you'll buy 'em to sell again.

L. MACD.   Thou speak'st with all thy wit, and yet, i' faith,
With wit enough for thee.

SON.   Was my father a traitor, mother?

L. MACD.   Ay, that he was.

SON.   What is a traitor?

L. MACD.   Why, one that swears and lies.

SON.   And be all traitors that do so?

L. MACD.   Every one that does so is a traitor, and must be hanged.

SON.   And must they all be hanged that swear and lie?

L. MACD.   Every one.

SON.   Who must hang them?

L. MACD.   Why, the honest men.

SON.   Then the liars and swearers are fools; for there are liars and
swearers enow to beat the honest men and hang up them.

L. MACD.   Now, God help thee, poor monkey! But how wilt thou do for
a father?

SON.   If he were dead, you'ld weep for him: if you would not, it were
a good sign that I should quickly have a new father.

L. MACD.   Poor prattler, how thou talk'st!

Enter a Messenger.

MESS.   Bless you, fair dame! I am not to you known,
Though, in your state of honour I am perfect.[4]
I doubt[5] some danger does approach you nearly:
If you will take a homely man's advice,
Be not found here; hence, with your little ones.
To fright you thus, methinks I am too savage;
To do worse to you were fell cruelty,
Which is too nigh your person. Heaven preserve you!
I dare abide no longer.   *Exit.*

L. MACD.   Whither should I fly?

---

[4] *perfect*] fully aware.
[5] *doubt*] fear.

I have done no harm. But I remember now
I am in this earthly world, where to do harm
Is often laudable, to do good sometime
Accounted dangerous folly: why then, alas,
Do I put up that womanly defence,
To say I have done no harm?—What are these faces?

Enter Murderers.

FIRST MUR.   Where is your husband?
L. MACD.   I hope, in no place so unsanctified
          Where such as thou mayst find him.
FIRST MUR.   He's a traitor.
SON.   Thou liest, thou shag-ear'd villain!
FIRST MUR.   What, you egg!
                                          [*Stabbing him.*
          Young fry of treachery!
SON.   He has kill'd me, mother:
          Run away, I pray you!   [*Dies.*
                        [*Exit Lady Macduff, crying* 'Murder!'
                        [*Exeunt murderers, following her.*

SCENE III. *England. Before the King's palace.*

Enter MALCOLM *and* MACDUFF.

MAL.   Let us seek out some desolate shade, and there
        Weep our sad bosoms empty.
MACD.   Let us rather
        Hold fast the mortal sword, and like good men
        Bestride our down-fall'n birthdom:[1] each new morn
        New widows howl, new orphans cry, new sorrows
        Strike heaven on the face, that it resounds
        As if it felt with Scotland and yell'd out
        Like syllable of dolour.

---

[1] *birthdom*] motherland.

MAL.   What I believe, I'll wail;
What know, believe; and what I can redress,
As I shall find the time to friend, I will.
What you have spoke, it may be so perchance.
This tyrant, whose sole name blisters our tongues,
Was once thought honest: you have loved him well;
He hath not touch'd you yet. I am young; but something
You may deserve of him through me; and wisdom
To offer up a weak, poor, innocent lamb
To appease an angry god.

MACD.   I am not treacherous.

MAL.   But Macbeth is.
A good and virtuous nature may recoil
In an imperial charge.[2] But I shall crave your pardon;
That which you are, my thoughts cannot transpose:[3]
Angels are bright still, though the brightest fell:
Though all things foul would wear the brows of grace,
Yet grace must still look so.

MACD.   I have lost my hopes.

MAL.   Perchance even there where I did find my doubts.
Why in that rawness[4] left you wife and child,
Those precious motives, those strong knots of love,
Without leave-taking? I pray you,
Let not my jealousies[5] be your dishonours,
But mine own safeties. You may be rightly just,
Whatever I shall think.

MACD.   Bleed, bleed, poor country:
Great tyranny, lay thou thy basis sure,
For goodness dare not check thee: wear thou thy wrongs;
The title is affeer'd.[6] Fare thee well, lord:
I would not be the villain that thou think'st
For the whole space that's in the tyrant's grasp
And the rich East to boot.

MAL.   Be not offended:

---

[2] *charge*] command.
[3] *transpose*] alter.
[4] *rawness*] exposed condition.
[5] *jealousies*] suspicions.
[6] *affeer'd*] confirmed.

I speak not as in absolute fear of you.
I think our country sinks beneath the yoke;
It weeps, it bleeds, and each new day a gash
Is added to her wounds: I think withal
There would be hands uplifted in my right;
And here from gracious England[7] have I offer
Of goodly thousands: but for all this,
When I shall tread upon the tyrant's head,
Or wear it on my sword, yet my poor country
Shall have more vices than it had before,
More suffer and more sundry ways than ever,
By him that shall succeed.

MACD.   What should he be?

MAL.   It is myself I mean: in whom I know
All the particulars of vice so grafted
That, when they shall be open'd, black Macbeth
Will seem as pure as snow, and the poor state
Esteem him as a lamb, being compared
With my confineless[8] harms.

MACD.   Not in the legions
Of horrid hell can come a devil more damn'd
In evils to top Macbeth.

MAL.   I grant him bloody,
Luxurious,[9] avaricious, false, deceitful,
Sudden,[10] malicious, smacking of every sin
That has a name: but there's no bottom, none,
In my voluptuousness: your wives, your daughters,
Your matrons and your maids, could not fill up
The cistern of my lust, and my desire
All continent[11] impediments would o'erbear,
That did oppose my will: better Macbeth
Than such an one to reign.

MACD.   Boundless intemperance

---

[7] *England*] the King of England.
[8] *confineless*] boundless.
[9] *Luxurious*] lascivious.
[10] *Sudden*] violent, impetuous.
[11] *continent*] restraining, chaste.

In nature[12] is a tyranny; it hath been
The untimely emptying of the happy throne,
And fall of many kings. But fear not yet
To take upon you what is yours: you may
Convey[13] your pleasures in a spacious plenty,
And yet seem cold, the time you may so hoodwink:
We have willing dames enough; there cannot be
That vulture in you, to devour so many
As will to greatness dedicate themselves,
Finding it so inclined.

MAL.   With this there grows
In my most ill-composed affection[14] such
A stanchless[15] avarice that, were I king,
I should cut off the nobles for their lands,
Desire his[16] jewels and this other's house:
And my more-having would be as a sauce
To make me hunger more, that I should forge
Quarrels unjust against the good and loyal,
Destroying them for wealth.

MACD.   This avarice
Sticks deeper, grows with more pernicious root
Than summer-seeming[17] lust, and it hath been
The sword of our slain kings: yet do not fear;
Scotland hath foisons[18] to fill up your will
Of your mere own: all these are portable,
With other graces weigh'd.[19]

MAL.   But I have none: the king-becoming graces,
As justice, verity, temperance, stableness,
Bounty, perseverance, mercy, lowliness,
Devotion, patience, courage, fortitude,
I have no relish[20] of them, but abound

---

[12] *nature*] natural appetites.
[13] *Convey*] carry out secretly.
[14] *affection*] disposition.
[15] *stanchless*] insatiable.
[16] *his*] one person's.
[17] *summer-seeming*] summer-like, transitory.
[18] *foisons*] rich harvests, plenty.
[19] *weigh'd*] counterbalanced.
[20] *relish*] trace.

                In the division[21] of each several crime,
                Acting it many ways. Nay, had I power, I should
                Pour the sweet milk of concord into hell,
                Uproar[22] the universal peace, confound
                All unity on earth.
MACD.   O Scotland, Scotland!
MAL.   If such a one be fit to govern, speak:
           I am as I have spoken.
MACD.   Fit to govern!
           No, not to live. O nation miserable!
           With an untitled tyrant bloody-scepter'd,
           When shalt thou see thy wholesome days again,
           Since that the truest issue of thy throne
           By his own interdiction stands accursed,
           And does blaspheme[23] his breed? Thy royal father
           Was a most sainted king: the queen that bore thee,
           Oftener upon her knees than on her feet,
           Died every day she lived. Fare thee well!
           These evils thou repeat'st upon thyself
           Have banish'd me from Scotland. O my breast,
           Thy hope ends here!
MAL.   Macduff, this noble passion,
           Child of integrity, hath from my soul
           Wiped the black scruples, reconciled my thoughts
           To thy good truth and honour. Devilish Macbeth
           By many of these trains[24] hath sought to win me
           Into his power; and modest wisdom plucks me
           From over-credulous haste: but God above
           Deal between thee and me! for even now
           I put myself to thy direction, and
           Unspeak mine own detraction; here abjure
           The taints and blames I laid upon myself,
           For strangers to my nature. I am yet
           Unknown to woman, never was forsworn,
           Scarcely have coveted what was mine own,

---

[21] *division*] variation.
[22] *Uproar*] disturb.
[23] *blaspheme*] slander.
[24] *trains*] stratagems, lures.

At no time broke my faith, would not betray
The devil to his fellow, and delight
No less in truth than life: my first false speaking
Was this upon myself: what I am truly,
Is thine and my poor country's to command:
Whither indeed, before thy here-approach,
Old Siward, with ten thousand warlike men,
Already at a point,[25] was setting forth.
Now we'll together, and the chance of goodness[26]
Be like our warranted quarrel! Why are you silent?

MACD. Such welcome and unwelcome things at once
'Tis hard to reconcile.

Enter a Doctor.

MAL. Well, more anon. Comes the king forth, I pray you?

DOCT. Ay, sir; there are a crew of wretched souls
That stay his cure: their malady convinces[27]
The great assay of art; but at his touch,
Such sanctity hath heaven given his hand,
They presently amend.

MAL.   I thank you, doctor.   [*Exit Doctor.*

MACD. What's the disease he means?

MAL.   'Tis call'd the evil:[28]
A most miraculous work in this good king;
Which often, since my here-remain in England,
I have seen him do. How he solicits heaven,
Himself best knows: but strangely-visited people,
All swoln and ulcerous, pitiful to the eye,
The mere[29] despair of surgery, he cures,
Hanging a golden stamp[30] about their necks,
Put on with holy prayers: and 'tis spoken,
To the succeeding royalty he leaves
The healing benediction. With this strange virtue
He hath a heavenly gift of prophecy,

[25] *at a point*] prepared.
[26] *goodness*] good fortune.
[27] *convinces*] conquers.
[28] *the evil*] i.e., the king's evil (scrofula).
[29] *mere*] absolute.
[30] *stamp*] coin.

> And sundry blessings hang about his throne
> That speak him full of grace.

Enter ROSS.

MACD.	See, who comes here?
MAL.	My countryman; but yet I know him not.
MACD.	My ever gentle cousin, welcome hither.
MAL.	I know him now: good God, betimes remove
	The means that makes us strangers!
ROSS.	Sir, amen.
MACD.	Stands Scotland where it did?
ROSS.	Alas, poor country!

Almost afraid to know itself! It cannot
Be call'd our mother, but our grave: where nothing,
But who knows nothing, is once[31] seen to smile;
Where sighs and groans and shrieks that rend the air,
Are made, not mark'd; where violent sorrow seems
A modern ecstasy:[32] the dead man's knell
Is there scarce ask'd for who; and good men's lives
Expire before the flowers in their caps,
Dying or ere they sicken.

MACD.	O, relation

Too nice,[33] and yet too true!

MAL.	What's the newest grief?
ROSS.	That of an hour's age doth hiss the speaker;
	Each minute teems a new one.
MACD.	How does my wife?
ROSS.	Why, well.
MACD.	And all my children?
ROSS.	Well too.
MACD.	The tyrant has not batter'd at their peace?
ROSS.	No; they were well at peace when I did leave 'em.
MACD.	Be not a niggard of your speech: how goes't?
ROSS.	When I came hither to transport the tidings,
	Which I have heavily borne, there ran a rumour
	Of many worthy fellows that were out;[34]

[31] *once*] ever.
[32] *modern ecstasy*] common emotion.
[33] *nice*] precise.
[34] *out*] in rebellion.

Which was to my belief witness'd the rather,
For that I saw the tyrant's power a-foot:
Now is the time of help; your eye in Scotland
Would create soldiers, make our women fight,
To doff their dire distresses.

MAL.   Be't their comfort
We are coming thither: gracious England hath
Lent us good Siward and ten thousand men;
An older and a better soldier none
That Christendom gives out.[35]

ROSS.   Would I could answer
This comfort with the like! But I have words
That would be howl'd out in the desert air,
Where hearing should not latch[36] them.

MACD.   What concern they?
The general cause? or is it a fee-grief[37]
Due to some single breast?

ROSS.   No mind that's honest
But in it shares some woe, though the main part
Pertains to you alone.

MACD.   If it be mine,
Keep it not from me, quickly let me have it.

ROSS. Let not your ears despise my tongue for ever,
Which shall possess[38] them with the heaviest sound
That ever yet they heard.

MACD.   Hum! I guess at it.

ROSS. Your castle is surprised; your wife and babes
Savagely slaughter'd: to relate the manner,
Were, on the quarry of these murder'd deer,
To add the death of you.

MAL.   Merciful heaven!
What, man! ne'er pull your hat upon your brows;
Give sorrow words: the grief that does not speak
Whispers the o'er-fraught heart, and bids it break.

MACD. My children too?

---

[35] *gives out*] proclaims.
[36] *latch*] catch.
[37] *fee-grief*] grief pertaining to an individual.
[38] *possess*] fill.

Ross.	Wife, children, servants, all
	That could be found.
Macd.	And I must be from thence!
	My wife kill'd too?
Ross.	I have said.
Mal.	Be comforted:
	Let's make us medicines of our great revenge,
	To cure this deadly grief.
Macd.	He has no children. All my pretty ones?
	Did you say all? O hell-kite! All?
	What, all my pretty chickens and their dam
	At one fell swoop?
Mal.	Dispute it like a man.
Macd.	I shall do so;
	But I must also feel it as a man:
	I cannot but remember such things were,
	That were most precious to me. Did heaven look on,
	And would not take their part? Sinful Macduff,
	They were all struck for thee! naught[39] that I am,
	Not for their own demerits, but for mine,
	Fell slaughter on their souls: heaven rest them now!
Mal.	Be this the whetstone of your sword: let grief
	Convert to anger; blunt not the heart, enrage it.
Macd.	O, I could play the woman with mine eyes,
	And braggart with my tongue! But, gentle heavens,
	Cut short all intermission; front to front
	Bring thou this fiend of Scotland and myself;
	Within my sword's length set him; if he 'scape,
	Heaven forgive him too!
Mal.	This tune goes manly.
	Come, go we to the king; our power[40] is ready;
	Our lack is nothing but our leave.[41] Macbeth
	Is ripe for shaking, and the powers above
	Put on their instruments. Receive what cheer you may;
	The night is long that never finds the day. [*Exeunt.*

---

[39] *naught*] wicked.
[40] *power*] army.
[41] *leave*] leave-taking.

ACT V.

SCENE I. *Dunsinane. Ante-room in the castle.*

Enter a Doctor of Physic *and a* Waiting-Gentlewoman.

DOCT. I have two nights watched with you, but can perceive no truth in your report. When was it she last walked?

GENT. Since his majesty went into the field, I have seen her rise from her bed, throw her nightgown upon her, unlock her closet, take forth paper, fold it, write upon't, read it, afterwards seal it, and again return to bed; yet all this while in a most fast sleep.

DOCT. A great perturbation in nature, to receive at once the benefit of sleep and do the effects of watching! In this slumbery agitation, besides her walking and other actual performances, what, at any time, have you heard her say?

GENT. That, sir, which I will not report after her.

DOCT. You may to me, and 'tis most meet you should.

GENT. Neither to you nor any one, having no witness to confirm my speech.

Enter LADY MACBETH, *with a taper.*

Lo you, here she comes! This is her very guise, and, upon my life, fast asleep. Observe her; stand close.[1]

DOCT. How came she by that light?

GENT. Why, it stood by her: she has light by her continually; 'tis her command.

DOCT. You see, her eyes are open.

GENT. Ay, but their sense is shut.

DOCT. What is it she does now? Look, how she rubs her hands.

---

[1] *close*] hidden.

69

GENT.   It is an accustomed action with her, to seem thus washing her
        hands: I have known her continue in this a quarter of an
        hour.

LADY M. Yet here's a spot.

DOCT.   Hark! she speaks: I will set down what comes from her, to
        satisfy my remembrance the more strongly.

LADY M. Out, damned spot! out, I say! One: two: why, then 'tis time to
        do't. Hell is murky. Fie, my lord, fie! a soldier, and afeard?
        What need we fear who knows it, when none can call our
        power to account? Yet who would have thought the old man
        to have had so much blood in him?

DOCT.   Do you mark that?

LADY M. The thane of Fife had a wife; where is she now? What, will
        these hands ne'er be clean? No more o' that, my lord, no
        more o' that: you mar all with this starting.

DOCT.   Go to, go to; you have known what you should not.

GENT.   She has spoke what she should not, I am sure of that: heaven
        knows what she has known.

LADY M. Here's the smell of the blood still: all the perfumes of Arabia
        will not sweeten this little hand. Oh, oh, oh!

DOCT.   What a sigh is there! The heart is sorely charged.

GENT.   I would not have such a heart in my bosom for the dignity[2] of
        the whole body.

DOCT.   Well, well, well,—

GENT.   Pray God it be, sir.

DOCT.   This disease is beyond my practice:[3] yet I have known those
        which have walked in their sleep who have died holily in
        their beds.

LADY M. Wash your hands; put on your nightgown; look not so pale: I
        tell you yet again, Banquo's buried; he cannot come out on's
        grave.

DOCT.   Even so?

LADY M. To bed, to bed; there's knocking at the gate: come, come, come,
        come, give me your hand: what's done cannot be undone: to
        bed, to bed, to bed.   [*Exit.*

DOCT.   Will she go now to bed?

GENT.   Directly.

---

[2] *dignity*] worth.
[3] *practice*] art, skill.

DOCT.   Foul whisperings are abroad: unnatural deeds
          Do breed unnatural troubles: infected minds
          To their deaf pillows will discharge their secrets:
          More needs she the divine than the physician.
          God, God forgive us all! Look after her;
          Remove from her the means of all annoyance,[4]
          And still keep eyes upon her. So good night:
          My mind she has mated[5] and amazed my sight:
          I think, but dare not speak.

GENT.   Good night, good doctor. [*Exeunt.*

SCENE II. *The country near Dunsinane.*

Drum and colours. Enter MENTEITH, CAITHNESS, ANGUS, LENNOX, *and* Soldiers.

MENT.   The English power is near, led on by Malcolm,
          His uncle Siward and the good Macduff:
          Revenges burn in them; for their dear causes
          Would to the bleeding and the grim alarm
          Excite the mortified man.

ANG.   Near Birnam wood
          Shall we well meet them; that way are they coming.

CAITH.   Who knows if Donalbain be with his brother?

LEN.   For certain, sir, he is not: I have a file[1]
          Of all the gentry: there is Siward's son,
          And many unrough[2] youths, that even now
          Protest[3] their first of manhood.

MENT.   What does the tyrant?

---

[4] *annoyance*] injury.
[5] *mated*] confounded.

---

[1] *file*] list.
[2] *unrough*] unbearded.
[3] *protest*] proclaim.

CAITH.   Great Dunsinane he strongly fortifies:
    Some say he's mad; others, that lesser hate him,
    Do call it valiant fury: but, for certain,
    He cannot buckle his distemper'd cause
    Within the belt of rule.

ANG.   Now does he feel
    His secret murders sticking on his hands;
    Now minutely[4] revolts upbraid his faith-breach;
    Those he commands move only in command,
    Nothing in love: now does he feel his title
    Hang loose about him, like a giant's robe
    Upon a dwarfish thief.

MENT.   Who then shall blame
    His pester'd senses to recoil and start,
    When all that is within him does condemn
    Itself for being there?

CAITH.   Well, march we on,
    To give obedience where 'tis truly owed:
    Meet we the medicine of the sickly weal,
    And with him pour we, in our country's purge,
    Each drop of us.

LEN.   Or so much as it needs
    To dew the sovereign flower and drown the weeds.
    Make we our march towards Birnam.   [*Exeunt, marching.*

SCENE III. *Dunsinane. A room in the castle.*

Enter MACBETH, Doctor, *and* Attendants.

MACB.   Bring me no more reports; let them fly all:
    Till Birnam wood remove to Dunsinane
    I cannot taint[1] with fear. What's the boy Malcolm?
    Was he not born of woman? The spirits that know
    All mortal consequences have pronounced me thus:

[4] *minutely*] continual.

[1] *taint*] be infected.

'Fear not, Macbeth; no man that's born of woman
Shall e'er have power upon thee.' Then fly, false thanes,
And mingle with the English epicures:
The mind I sway[2] by and the heart I bear
Shall never sag with doubt nor shake with fear.

Enter a Servant.

The devil damn thee black, thou cream-faced loon![3]
Where got'st thou that goose look?

SERV.   There is ten thousand—

MACB.   Geese, villain?

SERV.   Soldiers, sir.

MACB.   Go prick thy face and over-red thy fear,
Thou lily-liver'd boy. What soldiers, patch?[4]
Death of thy soul! those linen cheeks of thine
Are counsellors to fear. What soldiers, whey-face?

SERV.   The English force, so please you.

MACB.   Take thy face hence.   [*Exit Servant.*
                        Seyton!—I am sick at heart,
When I behold—Seyton, I say!—This push[5]
Will cheer me ever, or disseat me now.
I have lived long enough: my way[6] of life
Is fall'n into the sear, the yellow leaf,
And that which should accompany old age,
As honour, love, obedience, troops of friends,
I must not look to have; but, in their stead,
Curses, not loud but deep, mouth-honour, breath,
Which the poor heart would fain deny, and dare not.
Seyton!

Enter SEYTON.

SEY.   What's your gracious pleasure?

---

[2] *sway*] rule myself.
[3] *loon*] brute, rogue.
[4] *patch*] clown, fool.
[5] *push*] attack.
[6] *way*] course, term.

MACB.   What news more?
SEY.   All is confirm'd, my lord, which was reported.
MACB.   I'll fight, till from my bones my flesh be hack'd.
           Give me my armour.
SEY.   'Tis not needed yet.
MACB.   I'll put it on.
           Send out moe[7] horses, skirr[8] the country round;
           Hang those that talk of fear. Give me mine armour.
           How does your patient, doctor?
DOCT.   Not so sick, my lord,
           As she is troubled with thick-coming fancies,
           That keep her from her rest.
MACB.   Cure her of that.
           Canst thou not minister to a mind diseased,
           Pluck from the memory a rooted sorrow,
           Raze out the written troubles of the brain,
           And with some sweet oblivious antidote
           Cleanse the stuff'd bosom of that perilous stuff
           Which weighs upon the heart?
DOCT.   Therein the patient
           Must minister to himself.
MACB.   Throw physic to the dogs, I'll none of it.
           Come, put mine armour on; give me my staff.
           Seyton, send out. Doctor, the thanes fly from me.
           Come, sir, dispatch. If thou couldst, doctor, cast
           The water[9] of my land, find her disease
           And purge it to a sound and pristine health,
           I would applaud thee to the very echo,
           That should applaud again. Pull't off, I say.
           What rhubarb, senna,[10] or what purgative drug,
           Would scour these English hence? Hear'st thou of them?
DOCT.   Ay, my good lord; your royal preparation
           Makes us hear something.
MACB.   Bring it[11] after me.

---

[7] *moe*] more.
[8] *skirr*] move rapidly, scour.
[9] *cast The water*] inspect the urine.
[10] *senna*] Cassia senna, a plant used as a purgative.
[11] *it*] i.e., a piece of Macbeth's armor.

I will not be afraid of death and bane
Till Birnam forest come to Dunsinane.
DOCT.   [*Aside*] Were I from Dunsinane away and clear,
Profit again should hardly draw me here.   [*Exeunt*.

SCENE IV. *Country near Birnam wood*.

Drum and colours. Enter MALCOLM, *old* SIWARD *and his* Son, MAC-
DUFF, MENTEITH, CAITHNESS, ANGUS, LENNOX, ROSS, *and* Soldiers,
marching.

MAL.   Cousins, I hope the days are near at hand
That chambers will be safe.
MENT.   We doubt it nothing.
SIW.   What wood is this before us?
MENT.   The wood of Birnam.
MAL.   Let every soldier hew him down a bough,
And bear't before him: thereby shall we shadow
The numbers of our host, and make discovery
Err in report of us.
SOLDIERS.   It shall be done.
SIW.   We learn no other but the confident tyrant
Keeps still in Dunsinane, and will endure
Our setting down before't.
MAL.   'Tis his main hope:
For where there is advantage[1] to be given,
Both more and less have given him the revolt,
And none serve with him but constrained things
Whose hearts are absent too.
MACD.   Let our just censures
Attend the true event, and put we on
Industrious soldiership.

[1] *advantage*] opportunity.

SIW.　　　　　　　　　　　　The time approaches,
　　　　That will with due decision make us know
　　　　What we shall say we have and what we owe.
　　　　Thoughts speculative their unsure hopes relate,
　　　　But certain issue strokes must arbitrate:
　　　　Towards which advance the war.　　　　[*Exeunt, marching.*

SCENE V. *Dunsinane. Within the castle.*

Enter MACBETH, SEYTON, *and* Soldiers, *with drum and colours.*

MACB.　　Hang out our banners on the outward walls;
　　　　The cry is still 'They come': our castle's strength
　　　　Will laugh a siege to scorn: here let them lie
　　　　Till famine and the ague eat them up:
　　　　Were they not forced[1] with those that should be ours,
　　　　We might have met them dareful,[2] beard to beard,
　　　　And beat them backward home.　　　[*A cry of women within.*
　　　　　　　　　　　　　　　　　What is that noise?
SEY.　　It is the cry of women, my good lord.　　　　[*Exit.*
MACB.　　I have almost forgot the taste of fears:
　　　　The time has been, my senses would have cool'd
　　　　To hear a night-shriek, and my fell of hair[3]
　　　　Would at a dismal treatise[4] rouse and stir
　　　　As life were in't: I have supp'd full with horrors;
　　　　Direness,[5] familiar to my slaughterous thoughts,
　　　　Cannot once start me.

Re-enter SEYTON.

　　　　　　　　　　　　　Wherefore was that cry?
SEY.　　The queen, my lord, is dead.

---

[1] *forced*] reinforced.
[2] *dareful*] boldly.
[3] *fell of hair*] hairy skin.
[4] *treatise*] tale.
[5] *Direness*] horror.

MACB.   She should have died hereafter;
          There would have been a time for such a word.
          To-morrow, and to-morrow, and to-morrow,
          Creeps in this petty pace from day to day,
          To the last syllable of recorded time;
          And all our yesterdays have lighted fools
          The way to dusty death. Out, out, brief candle!
          Life's but a walking shadow, a poor player
          That struts and frets his hour upon the stage
          And then is heard no more: it is a tale
          Told by an idiot, full of sound and fury,
          Signifying nothing.

Enter a MESSENGER.

          Thou comest to use thy tongue; thy story quickly.
MESS.   Gracious my lord,
          I should report that which I say I saw,
          But know not how to do it.
MACB.   Well, say, sir.
MESS.   As I did stand my watch upon the hill,
          I look'd toward Birnam, and anon, methought,
          The wood began to move.
MACB.   Liar and slave!
MESS.   Let me endure your wrath, if't be not so:
          Within this three mile may you see it coming;
          I say, a moving grove.
MACB.   If thou speak'st false,
          Upon the next tree shalt thou hang alive,
          Till famine cling[6] thee: if thy speech be sooth,
          I care not if thou dost for me as much.
          I pull in resolution, and begin
          To doubt the equivocation of the fiend
          That lies like truth: 'Fear not, till Birnam wood
          Do come to Dunsinane'; and now a wood
          Comes toward Dunsinane. Arm, arm, and out!
          If this which he avouches does appear,
          There is nor flying hence nor tarrying here.
          I 'gin to be a-weary of the sun,

[6] *cling*] shrivel.

And wish the estate o' the world were now undone.
Ring the alarum-bell! Blow, wind! come, wrack!
At least we'll die with harness on our back.   [*Exeunt.*

SCENE VI. *Dunsinane. Before the castle.*

Drum and colours. Enter MALCOLM, *old* SIWARD, MACDUFF, *and their*
Army, *with boughs.*

MAL. Now near enough; your leavy screens throw down,
   And show like those you are. You, worthy uncle,
   Shall, with my cousin, your right noble son,
   Lead our first battle:[1] worthy Macduff and we
   Shall take upon's what else remains to do,
   According to our order.
SIW.   Fare you well.
   Do we but find the tyrant's power to-night,
   Let us be beaten, if we cannot fight.
MACD. Make all our trumpets speak; give them all breath,
   Those clamorous harbingers of blood and death. [*Exeunt.*

SCENE VII. *Another part of the field.*

Alarums. Enter MACBETH.

MACB. They have tied me to a stake; I cannot fly,
   But bear-like I must fight the course. What's he
   That was not born of woman? Such a one
   Am I to fear, or none.

Enter young SIWARD.

---

[1] *battle*] army.

Yo. Siw.	What is thy name?
Macb.	Thou'lt be afraid to hear it.
Yo. Siw.	No; though thou call'st thyself a hotter name
	Than any is in hell.
Macb.	My name's Macbeth.
Yo. Siw.	The devil himself could not pronounce a title
	More hateful to mine ear.
Macb.	No, nor more fearful.
Yo. Siw.	Thou liest, abhorred tyrant; with my sword
	I'll prove the lie thou speak'st.

                               [They fight, and young Siward is slain.

Macb.	Thou wast born of woman.
	But swords I smile at, weapons laugh to scorn,
	Brandish'd by man that's of a woman born. *[Exit.*

Alarums. Enter Macduff.

Macd.	That way the noise is. Tyrant, show thy face!
	If thou be'st slain and with no stroke of mine,
	My wife and children's ghosts will haunt me still.
	I cannot strike at wretched kerns,[1] whose arms
	Are hired to bear their staves:[2] either thou, Macbeth,
	Or else my sword, with an unbatter'd edge,
	I sheathe again undeeded. There thou shouldst be;
	By this great clatter, one of greatest note
	Seems bruited:[3] let me find him, fortune!
	And more I beg not. *[Exit. Alarums.*

Enter Malcolm *and old* Siward.

Siw.	This way, my lord; the castle's gently render'd:[4]
	The tyrant's people on both sides do fight;
	The noble thanes do bravely in the war;
	The day almost itself professes yours,
	And little is to do.
Mal.	We have met with foes

---

[1] *kerns*] Irish mercenaries.
[2] *staves*] spear shafts.
[3] *bruited*] reported.
[4] *gently render'd*] surrendered unreluctantly.

        That strike beside us.

Siw.   Enter, sir, the castle. [*Exeunt. Alarum.*

SCENE VIII. *Another part of the field.*

Enter MACBETH.

Macb.   Why should I play the Roman fool, and die
         On mine own sword? whiles I see lives, the gashes
         Do better upon them.

Enter MACDUFF.

Macd.   Turn, hell-hound, turn!
Macb.   Of all men else I have avoided thee:
         But get thee back; my soul is too much charged
         With blood of thine already.
Macd.   I have no words:
         My voice is in my sword, thou bloodier villain
         Than terms can give thee out!   [*They fight.*
Macb.   Thou losest labour:
         As easy mayst thou the intrenchant[1] air
         With thy keen sword impress as make me bleed:
         Let fall thy blade on vulnerable crests;
         I bear a charmed life, which must not yield
         To one of woman born.
Macd.   Despair thy charm,
         And let the angel whom thou still hast served
         Tell thee, Macduff was from his mother's womb
         Untimely ripp'd.
Macb.   Accursed be that tongue that tells me so,
         For it hath cow'd my better part of man!
         And be these juggling fiends no more believed,
         That palter[2] with us in a double sense;
         That keep the word of promise to our ear,

[1] *intrenchant*] invulnerable.
[2] *palter*] shuffle, equivocate.

	And break it to our hope. I'll not fight with thee.
MACD.	Then yield thee, coward,
	And live to be the show and gaze o' the time:
	We'll have thee, as our rarer monsters are,
	Painted upon a pole, and underwrit,
	'Here may you see the tyrant.'
MACB.	I will not yield,
	To kiss the ground before young Malcolm's feet,
	And to be baited with the rabble's curse.
	Though Birnam wood be come to Dunsinane,
	And thou opposed, being of no woman born,
	Yet I will try the last: before my body
	I throw my warlike shield: lay on, Macduff;
	And damn'd be him that first cries 'Hold, enough!'

                                        [*Exeunt, fighting. Alarums.*

Retreat. Flourish. Enter, with drum and colours, MALCOLM, *old* SIWARD, ROSS, *the other* Thanes, *and* Soldiers.

MAL.	I would the friends we miss were safe arrived.
SIW.	Some must go off: and yet, by these I see,
	So great a day as this is cheaply bought.
MAL.	Macduff is missing, and your noble son.
ROSS.	Your son, my lord, has paid a soldier's debt:
	He only lived but till he was a man;
	The which no sooner had his prowess confirm'd
	In the unshrinking station where he fought,
	But like a man he died.
SIW.	Then he is dead?
ROSS.	Ay, and brought off the field: your cause of sorrow
	Must not be measured by his worth, for then
	It hath no end.
SIW.	Had he his hurts before?
ROSS.	Ay, on the front.
SIW.	Why then, God's soldier be he!
	Had I as many sons as I have hairs,
	I would not wish them to a fairer death:
	And so his knell is knoll'd.
MAL.	He's worth more sorrow,
	And that I'll spend for him.

SIW.   He's worth no more:
      They say he parted well and paid his score:
      And so God be with him! Here comes newer comfort.

Re-enter MACDUFF, *with* MACBETH'S *head.*

MACD.   Hail, king! for so thou art: behold, where stands
      The usurper's cursed head: the time is free:
      I see thee compass'd with thy kingdom's pearl,
      That speak my salutation in their minds;
      Whose voices I desire aloud with mine:
      Hail, King of Scotland!

ALL.   Hail, King of Scotland!   [*Flourish.*
MAL.   We shall not spend a large expense of time
      Before we reckon with your several loves,
      And make us even with you. My thanes and kinsmen,
      Henceforth be earls, the first that ever Scotland
      In such an honour named. What's more to do,
      Which would be planted newly with the time,
      As calling home our exiled friends abroad
      That fled the snares of watchful tyranny,
      Producing forth the cruel ministers
      Of this dead butcher and his fiend-like queen,
      Who, as 'tis thought, by self and violent hands
      Took off her life; this, and what needful else
      That calls upon us, by the grace of Grace
      We will perform in measure, time and place:
      So thanks to all at once and to each one,
      Whom we invite to see us crown'd at Scone.
                                    [*Flourish. Exeunt.*

Study Guide

Text by
Rebecca McKinlay Sheinberg
(B.A., University of St. Thomas)

Department of English
Contemporary Learning Center High School
Houston, Texas

Contents

Section One: *Introduction* 87

   The Life and Work of William Shakespeare............ 87

   Historical Background 89

   Shakespearean Theatre.. 90

   Master List of Characters... 92

   Summary of the Play... 93

   Estimated Reading Time.. 95

> **Each scene includes List of Characters,
> Summary, Analysis, Study Questions and
> Answers, and Suggested Essay Topics.**

Section Two: *Act I* 96

   Scene I...96

   Scene II..97

   Scene III 97

   Scene IV...98

   Scene V 99

   Scene VI...99

   Scene VII...99

Section Three: *Act II* 107
   Scene I 107
   Scene II 108
   Scene III 109
   Scene IV 109

Section Four: *Act III* 117
   Scene I 117
   Scene II 117
   Scene III 118
   Scene IV 118
   Scene V 119
   Scene VI 119

Section Five: *Act IV* 124
   Scene I 124
   Scene II 125
   Scene III 125

Section Six: *Act V* 130
   Scene I 130
   Scene II 131
   Scene III 131
   Scene IV 131
   Scene V 131
   Scenes VI–VIII 132

Section Seven: *Bibliography* 138

Introduction

The Life and Work of William Shakespeare

William Shakespeare (1564–1616) is generally considered to be the greatest playwright and poet that has ever lived. His appeal is universal and his works have been translated, read, and analyzed throughout the world. Shakespeare wrote 154 sonnets, many poems, and 37 plays which have been grouped into comedies, histories, and tragedies.

Shakespeare's plays combine natural human conflict with dramatic flair producing entertainment that appeals to the audiences of today as well as the audiences for which they were written. Shakespeare understood human nature, and he created characters that portrayed human tragedy and human comedy. Some of his characters were fantastic and unworldly, yet they brought to the stage the truth that mere mortals could not.

Shakespeare was born in Stratford-Upon-Avon, in England. The exact date of his birth is unknown; however, records indicate he was baptized on April 26, 1564, at Holy Trinity Church. Traditionally, a baby was baptized about three days after birth, which would make Shakespeare's birthday April 23, 1564.

His father, John Shakespeare, was from the yeoman class and his mother, Mary Arden, was from a higher class known as the gentry class. The marriage raised John's status in town and the Shakespeare family enjoyed prominence and success in Stratford. This is verified through John Shakespeare's landholding and his status as an alderman.

William was the third child of eight, and it can be assumed he attended the local grammar school in Stratford. School ran for nine hours a day, year-round, and strict discipline was enforced. Shakespeare probably attended school until he was 15, which was customary for the time.

Around this time, Shakespeare's father was experiencing financial difficulty, and William probably took a job to help the family. His father was a glover and dealer in commodities, and Shakespeare may have assisted his father in his business, but it is presumed Shakespeare worked in a variety of jobs.

At 18, Shakespeare had an affair with Anne Hathaway, who was eight years his senior. They married, and six months later they had a child. Susanna Shakespeare was born in May of 1583 and in 1585 twins, Hamnet and Judith, were born to the Shakespeares. Little is known of that period except that the twins were christened in February 1585.

Shakespeare's life became public record in 1592 through a pamphlet written by Robert Greene with criticism of Shakespeare's work as an actor as well as a playwright. After Greene's death, the letter appeared again. Almost as quickly as it appeared, Greene's publisher printed an apology to Shakespeare.

From 1592 to 1594 many public theaters were closed due to the plague, and Shakespeare wrote poems and sonnets during this period. In 1594, he became a shareholder in a company of actors known as the Lord Chamberlain's Men. From 1594 to 1608 he was completely involved in the theatre.

His time in the years 1608 to 1616 was divided between the theater and his family. Shakespeare's success as a playwright and shareholder afforded him the luxury of owning homes in London and Stratford. His son Hamnet died at the age of 11. Judith had three boys, but all died. His daughter Susanna had one child, Elizabeth, who had no children. The recorded date for Shakespeare's death is April 23, 1616. He is buried inside the Stratford parish church. Shakespeare's last direct descendant, his granddaughter, Elizabeth, died in 1670.

Historical Background

Shakespeare drew from many sources when he wrote—the *Holingshed Chronicles of England* was one of these. From this source he drew much of his historical knowledge, as Holingshed was the definitive historical source of that time. The story of Macbeth comes from this source. However, Shakespeare changed several characters to meet the theatrical purpose of the play. In Holingshed's account Macbeth is older than Duncan, but Shakespeare reverses their ages and Duncan is portrayed as the older of the two.

Macbeth was written especially for James I and was performed in 1606. James I was King of Scotland when he came to the English throne; his descendants can be traced back to Banquo. In Shakespeare's Macbeth, often referred to in theater circles as "The Scottish Play," Banquo is portrayed as an honorable man who promotes goodness and fairness. In this way, Shakespeare was keenly aware of his audience and his political responsibilities. His plays reflect not only timeless conflicts and resolutions, but a view of the Elizabethan society.

The society in which Shakespeare lived was reflected in the characters he wrote about. London was a crowded city teaming with aristocrats, working class people, and indigents—it was a hub of activity. By today's standards the sanitation was very poor, and there were frequent epidemics of the plague. The city was infested with rats, and the fleas on the rats caused the Bubonic plague. There were no sewers, only open drains in the middle of the street. The conditions were difficult; however, the spirit of the people prevailed. It was in this society that Shakespeare wrote and created his characters.

Shakespearean Theatre

The support of theatre in England varied depending on who was the reigning monarch. Queen Elizabeth I (1533–1603) was the monarch when Shakespeare came into the public eye. Elizabeth supported the theater and the company performed at the castle on a regular basis. She reigned until her death in 1603 when James I became ruler.

James I was also an avid supporter of the theatre. Shakespeare's company, "Lord Chamberlain's Men," came under royal patronage and were subsequently known as "the King's Men." However, the local London government felt that actors and theater were improper. Therefore, no theaters were allowed to be built within the city limits. These restrictions did not keep the London people from the theaters, however, and by 1600 there were more theaters than ever built on the outskirts of London.

The Globe theater was built by Cuthbert Burbage in 1599 for the Lord Chamberlain's Men. When Burbage could not obtain a lease for the original theater, it was moved to a new site in Southwark, on the south side of the Thames River. The construction of the Globe was a joint venture between the Burbage brothers and the actors of the Lord Chamberlain's Men.

The Globe was a three-story structure with at least five sides and no roof over the stage. The roof extended around the gallery that encircled the theatre. Each floor had seats that encircled a stage that was built in the center. Behind the stage were dressing rooms and space to store scenery and props. There were no curtains used to conceal the stage, only a curtain to separate the backstage area from the stage. Very few props were used. In the front center portion of the stage was a trap door used to enable a person to vanish (or to allow a ghost to appear.)

A flag was flown from the front portion of the roof to announce when a play was to be presented. When patrons saw the flag, they knew there would be a performance that day; there were no performances at night, as there was no artificial lighting at the Globe. The theater was small—approximately 30 feet in height, 86 feet in diameter, 56 feet for the open courtyard, and about 40 feet for the stage itself. The patrons either stood in the courtyard and watched the play, or paid more and sat in the gallery.

The actors were flexible and dedicated to the craft of acting. They actors had a major responsibility to convey the purpose of the drama to the audience. The actors supported the written word through their portrayal of the characters. The dialogue and the language supported the setting of the scene within the play, as scenery was very limited. Shakespeare's language provided the scenery for the play. When the scene was changed to an evening scene, the actor would carry a torch in to indicate that it was night. The audience of the time was accustomed to this type of staging.

The theater was a much more intimate setting than the theaters of today. The patrons would voice their opinions during a production of a play; some even threw vegetables at the actors on the stage. The theater gained a reputation for rowdy behavior and aristocratic society did not consider theater a respectable part of Elizabethan society.

The Globe burned down in a fire in 1613, when a cannon was fired during a performance and the thatched roof over the gallery caught on fire. It was rebuilt that year, but in 1644 the structure was torn down when theatres were closed due to the government ban on theatres.

Master List of Characters

Three Witches—*Evil prophets that guide Macbeth's destiny with incomplete information regarding his future*

Macbeth—*Thane of Glamis, later King of Scotland*

Lady Macbeth—*Macbeth's wife and supporter of her husband's quest for power*

Duncan—*King of Scotland*

Malcolm—*Duncan's older son*

Donalbain—*Duncan's younger son*

Banquo—*General in the Scottish Army and Macbeth's friend*

Fleance—*Banquo's son who is seen as a threat by Macbeth*

Macduff—*Nobleman of Scotland and rival of Macbeth*

Lady Macduff—*Macduff's wife*

Son—*Macduff's son*

Lennox and Ross—*Noblemen of Scotland that support Malcolm's fight against Macbeth*

Angus—*Nobleman of Scotland and supporter against Macbeth*

Menteith and Caithness—*Noblemen of Scotland in Malcolm's English Army*

Porter—*servant at Macbeth's castle*

Murderers—*Macbeth's hired killers*

Hecate—*Goddess of the Witches*

Apparitions—*Visions conjured up by the Witches to inform Macbeth of what he should fear for the future*

Doctor and Gentlewoman—*Servants that witness Lady Macbeth's sleepwalking*

Seyton—*An Officer in Macbeth's Army*

Siward—*General in the English army fighting with Malcolm*

Young Siward—*Siward's son in the English army with Malcolm*

Captain—*Soldier in Duncan's military that reports on Macbeth's success in the battle against Macdonwald*

Summary of the Play

The play begins on an open stretch of land in medieval Scotland. Three Witches enter and give the prophecy that the civil war will end that day and that at sunset they will meet Macbeth. The Witches are summoned to leave, but they do not leave without stating that what is normally "fair" will be "foul," and what is "foul" will be "fair."

King Duncan learns that Macbeth has been victorious and has defeated Macdonwald. The Thane of Cawdor has betrayed Duncan and is accused of being a traitor. Duncan orders the Thane of Cawdor's execution and announces that Macbeth will receive the title of Thane of Cawdor.

Macbeth and Banquo leave the battlefield and meet the Witches. The Witches state the prophecy that Macbeth will be Thane of Cawdor and king and that Banquo will be the father of kings, but not king himself. Macbeth has been victorious on the battlefield and the war is at an end—to what greatness should he now aspire?

The Witches spark the ambitious nature in Macbeth, as he knows his rise to power would greatly be enhanced by being named Thane of Cawdor. After the Witches vanish, Ross and Angus arrive and announce that Macbeth has been named Thane of Cawdor. Banquo is skeptical of the Witches, but Macbeth, driven by a desire for power, considers killing Duncan to gain the crown. Macbeth is overwhelmed by the image, yet his desire for power is still present, as stated in a letter he sends to Lady Macbeth.

Lady Macbeth encourages Macbeth to act on his thoughts, telling him that she will guide and support his plan to kill King Duncan. While Duncan is visiting Inverness, Macbeth's castle, Macbeth kills Duncan as he sleeps. After the murder is discovered, Macbeth kills the servants, whom he accuses of Duncan's murder. Duncan's sons, fearing for their own lives, flee Scotland. Macbeth is crowned king.

Banquo raises suspicions that Macbeth killed Duncan. Macbeth hires two men to kill Banquo and his son Fleance, whom Macbeth fears will become king, as the Witches foretold. Banquo is killed, but Fleance escapes.

The Witches conjure a spell, and Apparitions reveal to Macbeth three prophecies that will affect his future. He is told to beware of Macduff, that no man born of woman can harm him, and he will not be conquered until the forest at Birnam marches to Dunsinane. Macbeth is also shown a procession of kings with the last king looking in a mirror—the reflection is that of Banquo.

Macbeth orders Macduff's family to be murdered and leaves for England to confront Macduff. When Macduff hears of the massacre of his family he vows to seek revenge on Macbeth. He joins Malcolm in his quest to depose Macbeth.

The army proceeds in camouflage by carrying a branch from Birnam Wood into battle. Alarmed by this, Macbeth fears the Witches' prophecy will come true. Macbeth is told of Lady Macbeth's death by her own hands and he laments the nature of his life.

Macbeth fights Macduff, and Macbeth boasts that he cannot be killed by any man born of woman. Macduff informs Macbeth that he was surgically removed from his mother's womb and thus was not born of woman. Macduff kills Macbeth in battle and hails Malcolm as King of Scotland. Malcolm vows to restore Scotland to a peaceful country.

Estimated Reading Time

The time needed to read *Macbeth* depends on the familiarity of the reader with the language of the Elizabethan Era. A recorded version of the play would serve as a source for pronunciation and aid the reader with inflection and intent of the words.

Since Shakespeare wrote in blank verse, a form of unrhymed poetry, there is a rhythm to the reading that becomes easier to follow as the reader moves through the play. The estimated reading time is approximately 12 to 14 hours.

SECTION TWO

Act I
(pages 1–18)

New Characters:

Three Witches: *evil prophets; also known as the Weird Sisters*

Duncan: *King of Scotland*

Malcolm: *Duncan's son*

Captain: *a wounded Scottish-soldier*

Lennox: *nobleman of Scotland*

Ross: *nobleman of Scotland*

Macbeth: *Duncan's cousin and General in the military*

Banquo: *soldier and Macbeth's friend*

Angus: *nobleman of Scotland*

Lady Macbeth: *Macbeth's wife*

Summary

Scene I (page 1)

The play opens on a bleak and lonely stretch of land in Scotland. Three Witches report that the battle Macbeth is fighting will be over by sunset; they plan to meet with Macbeth on the barren battlefield, or "heath," at that time.

The setting is enhanced by an approaching thunder storm and three Witches foretelling of the evil they foresee for the future: "Fair is foul, and foul is fair," what is good will be bad and what is bad will be good.

Scene II (pages 1–4)

The king of Scotland, Duncan, learns of the events of the battle from the wounded Captain that has just returned from the battlefield. The Captain informs Duncan that Macbeth has defeated Macdonwald, the Norwegian army, and the Thane of Cawdor. Macbeth is reported to be brave and fearless. The Captain states the conflict was resolved by Macbeth. The King orders the immediate execution of the traitorous Thane of Cawdor and names Macbeth as the new Thane of Cawdor. Duncan sends Ross to announce this to Macbeth on the battlefield.

Scene III (pages 4–9)

The Witches are on the battlefield discussing the evil and disruptive deeds they have been doing. The First Witch had a disagreement with a sailor's wife because the wife would not give her any of the chestnuts she was eating. This angers the Witches and they decide to torture the woman's husband by creating a windstorm that will blow his ship to all points on the compass. The storm will be so intense he will not be able to rest. The first Witch says, "I'll drain him dry as hay." She then brags about the "pilot's thumb," or small bone, she has as a charm. The Witches hear a drum and the approach of Macbeth.

Macbeth and Banquo enter and are unaware of the Witches at first. Macbeth's first line in the play, "So foul and fair a day I have not seen," alludes to the initial prophecy of the Three Witches. Banquo then spies the Witches, but he is unable to determine if they are men or women: "You should be women, and yet your beards forbid me to interpret that you are so." The Witches then greet Macbeth with his current title, Thane of Glamis, and two titles he is yet to have, Thane of Cawdor and King. Macbeth is perplexed by their greeting because he knows that both the Thane of Cawdor and King are still alive.

Banquo, hearing such a good fortune for this friend, inquires as to his own fate. He is told that he will be lesser and greater than Macbeth; even though he will never be king, his sons will. The Witches then dissolve into the air, leaving Banquo to wonder if they were real or just an hallucination.

Ross and Angus greet them with the news that Macbeth has been named Thane of Cawdor by Duncan. Banquo and Macbeth are surprised and contemplate the evil nature of the Witches. Macbeth is eager for power; however, Banquo warns him of the evil nature of the Witches and that the outcome of his actions could be disastrous to him.

Scene IV (pages 9–11)

Duncan inquires if the Thane of Cawdor has been executed and expresses regret as to giving the order to have him killed. Macbeth enters and they exchange accolades. Duncan names his own son, Malcolm to succeed him as king. This creates a conflict for Macbeth as Malcolm is another obstacle to overcome toward his goal to succeed Duncan as king.

> The Prince of Cumberland! That is a step
> On which I must fall down or else o'erleap
> For in my way it lies. Stars, hide your fires;
> Let no light see my black and deep desires.

Duncan plans to visit Inverness, Macbeth's castle, and the scene ends with Macbeth leaving to prepare for Duncan's visit.

Scene V (pages 11–13)

Lady Macbeth has received a letter from Macbeth stating that he has been named Thane of Cawdor. The letter reveals his ambition to be king and the prophecy given by the Witches. Lady Macbeth discloses her ambitious nature and vows to help Macbeth succeed in his ambition to be crowned King. She receives word that King Duncan will be arriving soon and is perplexed because Macbeth has not informed her himself. Macbeth arrives and they concur that by any means he should be crowned King:

> Come, you spirits
> Thast tend on mortal thoughts, unsex me here
> And fill me from the crown to the toe top-full
> Of direst cruelty! Make thick my blood...

Lady Macbeth tells him he should be a gracious host and they will speak on the matter later that evening.

Scene VI (pages 14–15)

Duncan arrives with his entourage and Lady Macbeth welcomes him upon his arrival. Duncan is eager to meet with Macbeth as he and Lady Macbeth exchange greetings.

Scene VII (pages 15–18)

Macbeth gives a dinner for Duncan and his guests that evening. During the dinner, Macbeth leaves and begins to contemplate the plan he and Lady Macbeth have discussed. He struggles with his conscience and the fear of eternal damnation if he murders Duncan. This internal conflict is reinforced because Macbeth is Duncan's cousin, he is a beloved king, and Duncan is a guest in his home:

> First, as I am his kinsman and his subject,
> Strong both against the deed; then as his host,
> Who should against his murderer shut the door,
> Not bear the knife myself.

Lady Macbeth calls Macbeth a coward and implies that he is less than a man for faltering in his plan to murder Duncan. Her resolute desire and quest for power sway Macbeth to agree with her and he decides to go through with the plan.

Analysis

Introducing the play with the Witches in the first scene creates an evil tone and mysterious setting; something sinister is about to happen. Witches were traditionally thought of in Elizabethan times as evil and connected to devil's work. The supernatural was feared and respected. The Witches statement, "Fair is foul, and foul is fair", clearly depicts that the events in the play will be evil and destructive. The thunderstorm and filthy air reinforce the evil prediction of the Witches and clearly indicates to the audience that a conflict between man and nature/good and evil exists within the world of the play. Scene I creates the atmosphere of evil that will continue throughout the play.

Duncan is portrayed as a concerned and interested ruler. The Captain reports the events in the battle and he characterizes Macbeth as a worthy and loyal subject to Duncan. The King is filled with gratitude and respect for Macbeth and the Captain. Duncan's compassion, however, is limited to his loyal subjects, as he orders the Thane of Cawdor's execution immediately upon hearing of him being a traitor.

Macbeth's actions in battle, by contrast, are barbaric and aggressive. He not only killed the enemy, but he cut him from his navel to his mouth, and cut off the victims head and placed it on the "battlements." This scene reveals the historical data needed for the introduction of the conflicts Macbeth creates and faces in his struggle for power. At this point Macbeth is viewed as a noble, loyal subject fighting battles victoriously for the King and Scotland. However, his actions on the battlefield reveal him to be a ruthless killer.

The Witches begin Scene III exhibiting the powers they possess; however, they are limited in these powers. They can create situations that will cause destruction (such as the storm), but they lack the power to actually sink the sailor's ship. The audience can infer that Macbeth will create his own havoc because the prophecy made by the Witches comes true. The Witches guide Macbeth's fate through their statements. Macbeth states, "So foul and fair a day I have not seen," echoing the Witches' lines in the first scene of the play. This repetition links Macbeth to the Witches. The audience makes a logical connection that Macbeth will be linked to the evil conflict in the world of the play.

Macbeth and Banquo meet the Witches on the field, and the Witches greet Macbeth with three titles. As noted through Banquo's dialogue, Macbeth is clearly startled. Banquo is equally interested in what the future will hold for him. He learns that his sons will be kings, but for him— nothing.

When Duncan's men give Macbeth the news that he is to be the new Thane of Cawdor, Macbeth considers what the Witches have said and becomes concerned about their evil nature. He states his desire to be King, but he ponders over the cost. Banquo questions the evil nature of the Witches' and warns Macbeth to look closer at the Witches predictions before he acts on them.

Duncan feels he may have acted in haste in ordering the death of the first Thane of Cawdor. This demonstrates the king's compassionate character and conscience. Macbeth greets his cousin Duncan with respect and friendship knowing full well he is plotting to take control. When Duncan announces that his son Malcolm will succeed him as king, Macbeth outwardly supports Duncan's decision. However, he is disappointed and knows he must eliminate Duncan and his son Malcolm to become king. Macbeth now struggles with this conflict and ponders what fate may bring.

Out of love for her husband, Lady Macbeth hardens her heart in order to aid him in mudering Duncan. Unlike Macbeth, she pushes aside her conscience when she makes her decision: "Nor heaven peep through the blanket of dark / To cry "Hold, hold!" She also uses the love they share to lend courage when Macbeth falters. Macbeth's success, and therefore her own fate, lies in Macbeth carrying out his homicidal plot.

When Duncan arrives at Inverness his gentle and loving nature is reinforced. He is again seen as a caring King interested in his subjects. This creates empathy for the innocent Duncan, and the image of Macbeth as a loyal trustworthy friend to Duncan begins to change. Macbeth reveals that he has a conscience as he questions his motives for killing Duncan. However, Lady Macbeth questions his manhood, calls him a coward, and coaxes Macbeth to follow through with the plan. She knows Macbeth's weak points and uses them to bolster his convinction. Her desire for Macbeth to be king overcomes her basic human compassion and greed seduces her morality. Macbeth becomes victim to his selfish desire for power.

Study Questions

1. What atmosphere is established in Scene I?

2. How does Banquo describe the Witches when he first sees them upon the heath?

3. Macbeth is reported to be a valiant soldier in Act I. The line, "Till he unseamed him from the nave to th'chops And fixed his head upon our battlements", paints a different Macbeth. What can you infer from that line?

4. In Scene I the Witches say, "Foul is fair and fair is foul." Which characters do you consider fair or foul?

5. Why do you think Shakespeare opened SceneIII with the Witches discussing an evil deed they have committed?

6. What prophesies do the Witches make for Macbeth and Banquo?

7. What does Lady Macbeth mean when she says of Macbeth, "Yet do I fear thy nature. It is too full o' the milk of human kindness To catch the nearest way"?

8. Macbeth is having second thoughts about killing Duncan. What are the reasons he gives? Based on these reasons what does he decide?

9.   What does Lady Macbeth mean when she says, "Was hope drunk Wherein you dressed yourself? Hath it slept since? And wakes it now to look so green and pale"?

10. What decision does Macbeth make at the end of Act I? What has Lady Macbeth said to influence his decision?

Answers

1.   The scene is filled with Witches, thunder and lightning, which creates a dark and sinister atmosphere.

2.   He calls them "withered" and "wild" in their attire; "That they look not like the inhabitants o' the' earth;" and that they "should be women...yet [their] beards forbid [him] to interpret that [they] are so."

3.   Macbeth is a cold-blooded killer on the battlefield.

4.   The Witches are foul because they are evil. Macbeth and Banquo seem to be fair because of their loyalty and bravery. However, Macbeth reveals his plan to murder Duncan and his character is viewed differently. Lady Macbeth is foul. Macdonwald is foul because he is a traitor. The Captain and Duncan are fair because the Captain fought bravely and the King supports him and is compassionate regarding the Captain's injury.

5.   The Witches are capable of creating situations that are evil and destructive. However, their powers are limited as they cannot destroy, but they have the power to create an atmosphere where destruction can easily occur.

6. The Witches state that Macbeth will be Thane of Cawdor and King. They go on to tell Banquo that his son's will be kings.

7. Lady Macbeth feels that Macbeth is kind and he may not be able to overcome his fears to kill Duncan. She fears his conscience will override his ambition to be King.

8. Macbeth is torn between his ambition and his conscience. He gives several reasons why he should not kill Duncan: 1) Duncan is his cousin; 2) He is a loyal subject to the King; 3) Duncan is his friend; 4) Duncan has never abused his royal power; and 5) Duncan is a guest in his home. Based on these reasons, Macbeth decides not to follow through with the murder of Duncan.

9. Lady Macbeth is questioning Macbeth why he has changed his mind about killing Duncan. She is asking him what has happened to his ambition.

10. Lady Macbeth persuades Macbeth to follow through with the plan to murder Duncan. She calls him a coward and less than a man, prodding Macbeth to follow her plan. Macbeth agrees to murder Duncan that night.

Suggested Essay Topics

1. Macbeth struggles with his conscience and the fear of eternal damnation if he murders Duncan. Lady Macbeth's conflict arises when Macbeth's courage begins to falter. Lady Macbeth has great control over Macbeth's actions. What tactics does she use to gain control over him? Cite examples from Act I. Does she solve her conflict through her actions? Cite examples from Act I.

2. Shakespeare begins *Macbeth* with Witches talking
    on a barren stretch of land in a thunder storm. This
    creates a certain atmosphere and mood. What im-
    ages contributed to the evil atmosphere? Do you
    feel this mood continues through Act I? Did the
    actions and dialog of the main characters reinforce
    this atmosphere?

SECTION THREE

Act II
(pages 19–31)

New Characters:

Fleance: *Banquo's son*

Porter: *doorman for Macbeth*

Macduff: *nobleman of Scotland*

Donalbain: *Duncan's younger son*

Summary

Scene I (pages 19–21)

There is something in the air that disturbs Banquo and Fleance and they cannot sleep. As they discuss the reasons for their inability to sleep, Macbeth joins them. Banquo confesses that he has been dreaming about the prophecy the Witches told them and he is concerned about the evil nature of the Witches. Macbeth responds by saying, "I think not of them." Both agree to discuss the matter at a later date. Banquo and Fleance retire to their chambers to sleep.

As Macbeth, alone in the hall, contemplates the murder he is about to commit, a bloody dagger appears before him:

> Is this a dagger which I see before me,
> The handle toward my hand? Come let me clutch
> thee.
> I have thee not, and yet I see thee still...
> And on thy blade and dudgeon gouts of blood.

Macbeth is still hesitant about killing Duncan. Once he hears Lady Macbeth's signal, though, the ringing of the bell, he no longer delays and proceeds to Duncan's room.

Scene II (pages 21–24)

Lady Macbeth is filled with anticipation for Macbeth's safe return and the completion of Duncan's murder. Her fears surface when she is startled by a noise that turns out to be nothing more than an owl screeching. She is concerned that the plot may not be completed and that Macbeth will be discovered before Duncan is murdered.

Lady Macbeth reveals in a soliloquy that when she placed the daggers in Duncan's chamber she considered killing Duncan herself. However, Duncan looked too much like her father and she could not commit the act herself: "Had he not resembled / My father as he slept, I had done't."

When Macbeth returns he is distraught and regrets the murder he has committed. Macbeth reports to Lady Macbeth that as he stepped past Duncan's guards, he heard a voice cry, "Sleep no more! Macbeth hath murdered sleep." In his tormented state, Macbeth leaves the murder scene carrying the bloody daggers.

Lady Macbeth urges him to return the daggers and place them by the slain Duncan, but Macbeth refuses to return to the chamber. Lady Macbeth returns the daggers and stains her hands with Duncan's blood. They hear a knock and retire to their sleeping quarters before the Porter arrives at the door.

Scene III (pages 24–29)

Macduff and Lennox have arrived at Macbeth's castle at Inverness at daybreak. The Porter jokes and carries on with Macduff about his drinking and lack of success with women the night before as Macbeth joins them. Macduff leaves Lennox and Macbeth to discuss the violent storm they had the night before.

Macduff rushes back to the courtyard with the news that the king had been murdered. Macbeth and Lennox rush to the chamber and Macduff sounds the alarm. Macbeth confesses when he saw the slain Duncan he was filled with rage and murdered Duncan's guards. He felt they were the murderers because they were smeared with blood and had the daggers in their hands. Confusion and shock ensues and Lady Macbeth faints. Donalbain and Malcolm fear foul play has been committed by someone close to them: "Where we are, / There's daggers in men's smiles; the nea'er in blood, / The nearer bloody."

Donalbain says he will go to Ireland, while Malcolm agrees to go to England. They flee the castle in fear of their own lives while Macduff, Macbeth, and the others agree to meet to discuss the catastrophe.

Scene IV (pages 29–31)

The following day Ross and an old man discuss the strange events that have taken place. Ross says that Duncan's horses became enraged, broke out of their stalls, and ate each other. Other unnatural events are going on with the birds and the weather. They fear all of this has to do with Duncan's murder.

Macduff joins the discussion and it is revealed that Duncan's body has been taken to the family plot at Colmekill and Macbeth has been named to succeed Duncan as King. The coronation will take place at Scone. Ross plans to go to Scone and Macduff leaves for Fife, of which he is Thane. Macduff fears the worst is yet to come.

Analysis

The second act opens with Banquo and his son, Fleance, walking the halls at Inverness, unable to sleep. Banquo has been plagued by dreams of the Witches. As he walks with Fleance, he hands him the sword and dagger he is wearing. Shakespeare uses this scene to foreshadow Fleance's eventual assumption of his father's role. Symbolically, the torch is being passed from father to son.

Macbeth enters and is confronted by Banquo, who was unable to distinguish him in the dim light. Macbeth greets Banquo as "a friend." This is ironic because in the next act, Macbeth proves to be much less than a friend. They discuss the prophecies of the Witches, Banquo saying he has dreamed of them, while Macbeth says he has not thought at all about them. Yet, they are all Macbeth has thought about. Macbeth has planned the murder of the King because of the prophecies.

After Banquo and his son have departed, Macbeth sends his servant to tell his wife to strike the bell when his drink is ready. This is his signal to enter Ducan's chamber and kill him. As he waits, a vision of a dagger appears floating before him. He reaches for it, but is unable to grasp it. He thinks the dagger is a product of his "heat-oppressed brain." The dagger beckons Macbeth toward Duncan's room and it becomes covered in blood as Macbeth approaches the chamber of the sleeping King. Macbeth's conscience creates the vision of the dagger, either to halt his plans by revealing the horror of the act or, as Macbeth believes, to beckon him forward. But, if Macbeth's will were about to falter, Lady Macbeth's signal, the ringing of the bell, provides him with the courage to finish what he has started.

Lady Macbeth greatly anticipates the return of Macbeth from the murderous act. While she waits, she gathers strength from the knowledge that she has drugged the drinks of Duncan's servants. "That which hath made them drunk hath made me bold;/ What hath quenched them hath given me fire!" Because the servants will be unable to stop Macbeth, Lady Macbeth knows that their plot to eliminate the king will be unimpeded. Yet, the act of murder and a guilty conscience cause her to jump at the screeching of an owl. She then refers to the "fatal bellman," a man that rang a bell outside a condemned man's cell encouraging him to confess his sins. She is inferring that Duncan is a condemned man and should repent his sins. Also, she could be referring to Macbeth, as he will be a condemned man if he is caught committing the murder. Even if he is not caught, the murder of Duncan is a sin that condemns Macbeth's soul.

Lady Macbeth asked to be "unsexed" in an earlier scene so that she may have the necessary strength to support Macbeth in his quest for the throne. However, when she placed the daggers by the sleeping Duncan, she was unable to kill him because he looked too much like her father. Her conscience surfaced and she deferred to Macbeth to complete the evil plan.

Having killed Duncan, Macbeth returns to his wife's side in a dazed and confused state. He then tells his wife that as he approached Duncan, one of the servants cried out "Murder" in his sleep. This woke both the servants up. One then said "God bless us!" and the other "Amen!" He is concerned that he could not say "amen" in return. He wanted to, but he found the words stuck in his throat. Macbeth is unable to receive the blessing he desires because of the sin he is about to commit.

After he has killed Duncan, his conscience begins to project voices that he thinks the entire castle can hear. "Still it cried 'Sleep no more!' to all the house;/ 'Glamis hath murdered sleep, and therefore Cawdor/ Shall sleep no more; Macbeth shall sleep no more.'" Macbeth feels so guilty for the act that his mind projects voices that condemn him. He will no longer have the piece of mind that he had before the murder.

Lady Macbeth counsels her husband to ignore the voices that he thinks he has heard because dwelling upon them and the act he has just committed could drive him mad. She also tells him to return the bloody daggers to Duncan's room. Macbeth is unable to face his crime again. so Lady Macbeth takes the daggers back. She returns with her hands now covered with blood like her husband. By having Lady Macbeth handle the daggers and get blood on her hands, Shakespeare is showing that even though she never commits an act of murder, her participation in planning makes her just as guilty.

When they hear the knock at the door, both adjourn to their sleeping quarters to establish an alibi if someone should come looking for them. Macbeth again expresses his regret at killing Duncan when he says, "Wake Duncan with thy knocking! I would thou/ couldst!"

In order to give the audience a moment to recuperate from the heavy drama of the last scene, scene III opens with the comic banter of the porter at the door. He talks with Macduff about the effects of drinking on the body. But besides a bit of comedy, the scene also serves to establish a diabolical atmosphere around Macbeth's castle. The porter curses in the "name of Beelzebub." He does not call to God, instead he calls forth the name of the devil. He then hypothesizes as to who is knocking at the door. He names three people who would knock at the gates of Hell; a farmer that hanged himself, an equivocator that commits treason, and a tailor who steals cloth. He even talks about the people who walk the way to the "everlasting bonfire."

These references to Hell serve to show the audience that Macbeth is creating a Hell within Scotland.

Macbeth then enters and Macduff goes to wake the king. While he is gone, Lennox–who arrived with Macduff–tells Macbeth of the turbulent night. The woeful weather outside mimics the horrible events inside Macbeth's castle. Macduff then returns with the news of the king's murder. Macbeth, faking astonishment, rushes off with Lennox to see the body. He later claims to have slain the servants, whom he had implicated in the murder, in a fit of rage over their heinous deed. Lady Macbeth continues her charade by fainting at the news.

Duncan's sons, Malcolm and Donalbain, fear that the real killers were not the servants, but someone closer to them. They fear that whoever is ambitious enough to kill the king will come after them as well. "This murderous shaft that's shot/Hath not yet lighted, and our safest way/Is to avoid the aim." Malcolm flees to England and Donalbain to Ireland. Once they have fled Scotland, they are considered guilty in their own father's murder.

There is a time lapse between the last two scenes of the second act. The Old Man and Ross discuss the events that have transpired over the last few days. They talk of strange portents and how ambition is the ruin of men. The audience can infer that Macbeth's ambition will ruin him. This last scene also shows how Macbeth is still unable to look upon the body of Duncan. He goes to Scone to be crowned instead of Colmekill for the funeral.

Study Questions

1. What are Banquo's concerns about the Witches prophecy? What is Macbeth's response?

2. What does Macbeth see when Banquo and Fleance leave and what does he say about it?

3. What was Lady Macbeth unable to do in Duncan's chamber? Why?

4. What was Macbeth's reaction when he returned from Duncan's chamber? What did he say?

5. Who was sleeping in the second chamber? Why did Shakespeare include that information in the play?

6. Macbeth is unable to return to Duncan's chamber with the bloody daggers. Why do you think he fears going back?

7. What does Lennox say to Macbeth about the previous night?

8. Who discovers that Duncan has been murdered?

9. Why does Macbeth say he has murdered the guards?

10. Why do Donalbain and Malcolm leave? Where do they say they are going?

Answers

1. He has had bad dreams about the Witches and part of what they said has come true. Macbeth says he has not thought about them. Banquo would like to discuss the matter with Macbeth.

2. He sees a bloody dagger floating before him. He says that it is only a dream.

3. She was unable to kill Duncan because he looked like her father.

4. He was upset and feeling guilt. He said that "it was a sorry sight." He also stated that he had murdered sleep and he could not say amen when he needed to.

5. Donalbain was sleeping. This puts suspicion on him.

6. He cannot face the murder that he has committed. He feels too much guilt.

7. Lennox said that there was a bad storm and he has never seen one this fierce in his life.

8. Macduff discovers Duncan's slain body.

9. Macbeth says he murdered the guards because felt they killed Duncan. He was so angry and grief stricken he could not control his rage.

10. Donalbain and Malcolm because they fear for their own lives. Donalbain goes to Ireland and Malcolm goes to England.

Suggested Essay Topics

1. The Witches are characters that have a powerful impact on the play, but have very few lines. Banquo says that he cannot sleep because he is thinking about them. Macbeth says that he has not thought about them at all. How do the characters of Macbeth and Banquo differ and what influence have the Witches had on each character?

2. Macbeth is alone while Lady Macbeth returns the bloody daggers when he says, "Will all great Neptune's ocean wash this blood clean from my hand? No, this my hand will rather The multitudinous seas incarnadine, Making the green one red." Lady Macbeth returns will blood on her hands as well. What does the blood symbolize? Cite examples from the play.

SECTION FOUR

Act III

(pages 33–49)

New Characters:

Murderers: *hired killers*

Hecate: *a Witch*

Summary

Scene I (pages 33–37)

Banquo says that the prophecy has come true for Macbeth. He would like the prophecy the Witches made about his sons to come true also. Banquo feels that he must appear loyal to Macbeth, yet he does not trust him.

Macbeth questions Banquo as to his schedule for the day and says to Banquo to be sure and join them at the banquet that evening. Banquo and his son plan to go out riding for the day. Macbeth is worried that the prophecy of Banquo's sons being kings will come true. His reign will be barren if his sons do not succeed him. Macbeth hires two men to murder Banquo and Fleance.

Scene II (pages 38–39)

Lady Macbeth questions Macbeth as to his plans, but he does not inform her of the plan to kill Banquo and Fleance. She encourages Macbeth not to think about Banquo or the events that have taken place. Macbeth tells her not to worry.

Scene III (pages 40–41)

A third murderer joins the two Macbeth had hired in the previous scene. They wait along the path that Banquo and his son travel. As they approach, walking their horses, the murderers jump out. Banquo is killed, but Fleance is able to escape.

Scene IV (pages 41–46)

At the banquet, Macbeth learns that the murderers have not been entirely successful. They killed Banquo, but Fleance was able to escape. Macbeth takes joy in learning that Banquo is dead, because he cannot produce any more sons. He says he will deal with the matter of Fleance later.

As Macbeth is seated at the banquet table, the ghost of Banquo appears. This startles Macbeth and he responds to the vision. No one but Macbeth can see the ghost. Lady Macbeth assures her guests that Macbeth has had these attacks since he was a child and it will soon pass. She urges Macbeth to resume his role as host. As quickly as he offers his apology to his guest, the ghost appears again. Macbeth loses control and Lady Macbeth fears he will confess to the murder of Duncan. She asks her guest to leave quickly. The ghost disappears and Macbeth questions why Macduff did not attend the banquet. Macbeth feels he must consult with the Witches again to gain information about the future.

Scene V (pages 46–47)

Hecate is another Witch that Shakespeare introduces to the audience. Hecate is upset because the other Witches did not consul her before they spoke to Macbeth. Hecate assures them she will conjure a spell that will lead Macbeth to a disastrous fate. She sends them to cast the spell and prepare the charm, as Macbeth plans to visit them soon.

Scene VI (pages 47–49)

Lennox says to a Lord that he feels it is a pity that Banquo was killed. He goes on to imply that Macbeth is responsible for both Duncan's and Banquo's deaths; even though the general consensus is that Fleance killed his own father, as did Malcolm and Donalbain. Lennox does not believe either had anything to do with the deaths of their fathers. Macbeth has stolen Malcolm's birthright to be king and Malcolm is in England trying to secure an army to gain his birthright back. Macduff has gone to join in his effort. Lennox and the Lord hope that Malcolm will be successful in restoring peace to Scotland.

Analysis

Banquo says Macbeth has attained all the Witches said he would and at great cost to everyone; he feels his own prophecy should come true as well. The friendship between Banquo and Macbeth has been dissolved. Banquo no longer trusts his friend and must be cautious in his presence. Macbeth knows that all the Witches have said has come true and fears Banquo's prophecy will also come true.

Macbeth feels his own sons should succeed him, not Banquo's. Macbeth states his fears and concerns, yet, he does not inform Lady Macbeth of what he has planned.

Macbeth feels he must resolve this conflict and he hires murderers to kill Banquo and his son. He feels this will guarantee that his heirs will succeed him. Macbeth does not express remorse or concern over the planning of Banquo and Fleance's murder, as he did with Duncan's murder. By now, he is so blinded with ambition and power and will stop at nothing to secure his powerful position.

Lady Macbeth and Macbeth discuss the problems they are having even though they have achieved what they wanted. Macbeth feels he has the Banquo situation in hand and assures Lady Macbeth not to worry about it. They both agree that they must continue to hide their true feelings at the banquet. Macbeth says that evil deeds are made stronger through additional evil deeds.

The murderers leave open the possibility of the prophecy being fulfilled because they are unsuccessful with the ambush on Banquo and his son. Banquo is killed, but his son Fleance escapes. Macbeth must still face the fact that Fleance is alive, yet he is delighted that the source has been killed. He does not have to worry about additional sons, only Fleance himself.

This scene also introduces a third murderer. He says he was sent by Macbeth, yet there is no other mention of him in the play. There is much speculation as to the identity of the third murderer. When *Macbeth* is performed on stage, the third murderer is sometimes hooded so that his features cannot be seen.

At the feast, Macbeth's fears and guilt overpower him and he loses control over his inner thoughts. He sees Banquo's ghost. The vision is horrible and he speaks openly to the ghost. Lady Macbeth is unable to control Macbeth, yet she urges him to reign in his fears and remember his guests. Her attempts are futile and she fears he will confess to the murder of Duncan to all the guests. This is the first time Macbeth gives way to a public expression of his inner conflicts; which marks a turning point in the drama. Macbeth continues to manifest his guilt through the vision of the ghost he can only see, and Lady Macbeth asks the guests to leave quickly as Macbeth seems to be getting worse. She has completely lost control of Macbeth.

Almost as quickly as the guests leave, Macbeth's fears surface concerning Macduff's not attending the banquet. Macbeth is fearful that, "Blood, they say: blood will have blood." He is paranoid about everyone and what their behavior means. He must control the situation even if that means killing someone to secure his position and remain in power. Macbeth feels his only recourse is to consult with the Witches as to his fate as they seem to see into the future.

Hecate, the Mistress of the Witches, is agitated that she was not informed as to the events concerning Macbeth. She plans to contribute to his fate by creating a situation that will enable Macbeth to create his own demise. This creates drama and reinforces the power the Witches have in the play.

(The scene with Hecate is not thought to have been in the original text. This has led to speculation that Shakespeare did not write the scene.)

Study Questions

1. As Act III begins Banquo is reflecting on what has happened to Macbeth. What three events does he state and what does he hope for himself?

2. What reason does Macbeth give the Murderers for wanting Banquo killed? What reason does he give for not doing it himself?

3. Why do you think Macbeth does not tell Lady Macbeth about his plan to murder Banquo and Fleance?

4. When Banquo's ghost enters the banquet what is Macbeth's reaction?

5. What does Lady Macbeth say to the guest is the reason for his behavior?

6. Does Macbeth recognize the ghost? How do you know he does?

7. What does Hecate say she is going to do to Macbeth? Why does she think he will respond to her?

8. What does Lennox say about Malcolm, Donalbain, and Fleance?

9. Where has Macduff gone and why?

10. What does Lennox hope for?

Answers

1. Banquo says that Macbeth was made King, Thane of Cawdor and Thane of Glamis. He hopes his sons will be Kings.

2. Macbeth fears for his own life if Banquo lives. Macbeth says that he and Banquo have the same friends and Macbeth would not be able to remain friends with them if he killed Banquo himself.

3. Macbeth either feels that Lady Macbeth may try to talk him out the plot, or he wants to have full control and exclude her from this matter.

4. Macbeth questions who has brought Banquo to the feast and he is very upset.

5. Lady Macbeth tells them that he has suffered from this affliction his entire life and to ignore his behavior.

6. Macbeth recognizes Banquo and says to the ghost that he should not blame him for the murder, "Thou canst not say I did it: never shake Thy gory locks at me."

7. Hecate is going to create a situation that will allow Macbeth to ruin himself. The Witches will make a magic potion that will guide Macbeth's fate by telling him the future. Hecate says mortal men cannot resist knowing the future.

8. Lennox says they have been unjustly accused of murder.

9. Macduff has gone to England to join Malcolm's forces to overthrow Macbeth.

10. Lennox hopes that Scotland will be peaceful again.

Suggested Essay Topics

1. There is a turning point in Act III, Scene IV. What is that turning point and how do you think Macbeth will respond throughout the rest of the drama? Cite examples from the play.

2. Compare and contrast the murders of Banquo and Duncan. How does the murder of Banquo show the change in Macbeth?

SECTION FIVE

Act IV
(pages 51–67)

New Characters:

Apparitions: *visions created by the Witches*

Lady Macduff: *Macduff's distraught wife*

Son: *Macduff's child*

Summary

Scene I (pages 51–56)

The Witches are preparing a magic potion and casting a spell. They chant incantations three times to make sure the charm's power will be strong. Macbeth greets the Witches and demands that they give him information about the future. The Witches call upon Apparitions to inform Macbeth of his future.

The first Apparition is that of an armed head saying he should beware of Macduff. The second Apparition is that of a bloody child and it states that no man born of woman will harm Macbeth. The third Apparition is that of a crowned child holding a tree. This Apparition says, "Macbeth shall never vanquished be until Great Birnam Wood to high Dunsinane Hill shall come against him."

Macbeth urges the Witches to give him additional information about the future. The Witches show him a procession of kings and the last holding a mirror with the reflection of Banquo. The Witches disappear and Macbeth asks Lennox if he saw the Witches as he entered the room. Lennox said he did not. Lennox then informs Macbeth that Macduff has fled to England. Macbeth says he plans to kill Macduff's family.

Scene II (pages 56–59)

Lady Macduff is angered and enraged that her husband, Macduff, has left for England without telling her. She does not know what they are to do now. Ross tries to console her, but she feels her husband is a traitor and a coward. Macduff's son questions his mother about the father's disappearance. She tells him his father is dead; he does not believe her. A messenger arrives and warns Lady Macduff that her life is in danger and she must leave immediately. The Murderers arrive and kill Lady Macduff and her son.

Scene III (pages 59–67)

Malcolm and Macduff are in England. Malcolm questions Macduff's motives and wants to make sure that he has not been sent by Macbeth. Malcolm goes on to confess that he has many vices that may make him a far worse King than Macbeth. Macduff's response is that Malcolm is the rightful heir to the throne and Macbeth must be unseated at all cost. Malcolm is convinced that Macduff is sincere and says that the things he said about himself were not true. Malcolm says he is sincere and pure and seeks only good for Scotland.

Ross enters and informs Malcolm and Macduff that Scotland is in a terrible condition. At first Ross hesitates, but then informs Macduff that his family has been brutally murdered. Macduff is shocked and vows to revenge the murder of his family.

Analysis

Hecate knows that Macbeth will not question information given to him but will act upon it. Macbeth is given information that he feels will give him immortality. He is ready to believe only what he feels will benefit him, but he is unable to distinguish the "good" from the "bad". The "Fair is foul and the foul is fair" statement made by the Witches and by Macbeth in this drama has been reinforced in this Act.

Macbeth is no longer capable of making rational judgments or distinguishing good from evil. Obsessed with this knowledge, Macbeth feels he must take quick action to preserve his future. Macbeth feels he must seek Macduff and kill him and his family to insure that the blood line is stopped.

Macbeth is out of control and reacts without thought to his actions. He feels he must spill blood to remain in control and powerful. Once again Macbeth has innocent blood on his hands, and again, he feels no remorse. He is driven by his lust to control the situation and flex his power. The fact that Shakespeare allows the act of the murder to be witnessed as it occurs, rather than have it reported, gives the audience a first-hand impression of the evil nature of Macbeth. The senseless murder of Lady Macduff and her son contribute to Macbeth's demise and reinforces the flaws in his character.

Malcolm confesses to Macduff that his own character is far worse than Macbeth. He says he has committed crimes worse than Macbeth. Macduff states that he feels

Malcolm has the birthright to be the king of Scotland and he knows that he is worthy. Malcolm says that he was only testing Macduff's sincerity. Shakespeare uses this ploy to show that Malcolm is a good man and should be the king. The audience supports Malcolm's efforts to restore Scotland.

The murder of Macduff's family is unnecessary and the act of a tyrant. When Macduff learns that his family has been murdered, he is even more determined to seek revenge on Macbeth. Macbeth is seen as a barbaric killer and Malcolm's cause is reinforced by Macbeth's actions. The murder is the last event that Malcolm and Macduff can allow; they vow to overthrow Macbeth and reclaim Scotland for the people.

Study Questions

1. What are the Witches doing at the beginning of Act IV?

2. What are the three statements made by the Apparitions?

3. What is the significance of the Witches having the Apparitions give the information to Macbeth?

4. What does Macbeth decide to do with the information the Witches have given him?

5. What does Lady Macduff say is the reason for her husband leaving?

6. What does Lady Macduff tell her son about his father? How does he respond to her?

7. What happens to Lady Macduff and her son?

8. Why does Malcolm question Macduff?

9. What is Malcolm's reaction to the news? What is Macduff's?

10. What do Malcolm and Macduff plan to do?

Answers

1. The Witches are standing over a cauldron preparing a spell for Macbeth.

2. The Apparitions say: 1) That Macbeth should beware of Macduff, 2) That no man born of a woman can harm Macbeth, and 3) Macbeth will not be harmed unless Great Birnam Wood comes to high Dunsinane.

3. The Apparitions are dressed in such a way to give insight to Macbeth. He is blinded by his quest for power and does not recognize the significance of the appearance.

4. He plans on going to England to kill Macduff.

5. Lady Macduff feels her husband is scared and is a traitor.

6. Lady Macduff tells her son his father is dead. Her son does not believe her.

7. Lady Macduff and her son are murdered.

8. Malcolm wants to know if Macduff is sincere and that he has not been sent by Macbeth.

9. Malcolm is enraged by the news of Lady Macduff's death. Macduff is in shock at first then he vows to seek revenge against Macbeth.

10. Malcolm and Macduff plan on killing Macbeth and restoring the peace in Scotland.

Suggested Essay Topics

1. What is the symbolic purpose of each prophecy the Apparitions state in the play? What interpretation can be drawn from the way each are dressed. Do you feel there is a hidden meaning? Cite examples from Act IV.

2. Act IV, Scene II is the only scene Lady Macduff is in. Why do you feel Shakespeare chose to have the murder in the scene instead of having it reported, as with Duncan's murder?

SECTION SIX

Act V

(pages 69–82)

New Characters:

Gentlewoman: *a woman attending Lady Macbeth*

Doctor: *the physician in the castle*

Carthness and Menteith: *nobleman of Scotland in Malcolm's English Army*

Seyton: *an Officer in Macbeth's army*

Siward: *general in the English army fighting with Malcolm*

Young Siward: *Siward's son in the English army with Malcolm*

Summary

Scene I (pages 69–71)

The Gentlewoman reports to the Doctor that Lady Macbeth is sleepwalking and her behavior is very strange. The Gentlewoman says that Lady Macbeth gets out of bed, puts on a nightgown, unlocks her closet, writes on a piece of paper, seals the letter and returns to bed.

Lady Macbeth says things that the Gentlewoman refuses to repeat because she fears she will be charged with treason. She urges the Doctor to hear them for himself. The doctor watches Lady Macbeth and concludes that he cannot treat her illness as she needs the assistance of God. He is very concerned about Lady Macbeth's safety and tells the Gentlewoman to watch her closely.

Scene II (pages 71–72)

Menteith, Angus, Lennox and Caithness discuss the battle plans of Malcolm. They plan to meet near Birnam Wood with the others. Macbeth has secured Dunsinane, but his forces are not loyal subjects. Each vow to fight to the death to regain control of Scotland and overthrow Macbeth.

Scene III (pages 72–75)

Macbeth is secure in his castle at Dunsinane. He feels confident because the Witches told him that he cannot be harmed unless the prophecies come to pass. He believes the Witches and has no fear. Macbeth dresses for battle as the Doctor reveals Lady Macbeth's condition to him. He ask the Doctor to find a cure for his wife. Macbeth leaves for the battle.

Scene IV (pages 75–76)

Malcolm, Menteith, and Siward are near Birnam Wood. Malcolm tells them they should each cut a branch from a tree from Birnam Wood and use it as camouflage. They prepare to march on to Dunsinane.

Scene V (pages 76–78)

Macbeth feels confident that he will overthrow Malcolm in battle. Macbeth hears a cry and discovers that Lady Macbeth is dead. Macbeth responds by saying that life is very short. A messenger arrives to inform Macbeth that the wood of Birnam seems to be moving toward Dunsinane. Macbeth sounds the alarm and prepares to fight.

Scenes VI–VIII (pages 78–82)

Malcolm, Siward, and Macduff arrive at Dunsinane and enter Macbeth's castle. Macbeth and Young Siward have a fight and Young Siward is killed. Macduff comes face to face with Macbeth. Macbeth urges Macduff to leave, as Macbeth feels he has enough of Macduff's blood on his hands. Macbeth tells Macduff that he cannot be harmed and cannot be killed by any man born from a woman. Macduff informs Macbeth that he was not born of woman, but was "untimely ripped" from his mother's womb. Macbeth says that what the Witches said had a double meaning and he did not realize in time the meaning of their prophecy. Macduff calls Macbeth a coward and coerces Macbeth into fighting him. The two exit and continue their sword fight.

Siward is informed that his son has died valiantly in battle. Macduff returns with the severed head of Macbeth and proclaims Malcolm as the rightful heir to the throne. Malcolm assures the people that Scotland will be restored to a peaceful place when he is King. Malcolm vows to honor the Thanes and kinsmen that helped in the fight against Macbeth with the title of Earl. The drama ends with Malcolm inviting the victors to his coronation at Scone.

Analysis

Lady Macbeth's behavior has been very peculiar, according to the Gentlewoman, and the Doctor is summoned to witness the behavior for himself. Lady Macbeth is responding to her guilty feelings. She is trying to rid herself of her guilt, which takes the form of the blood she is unable to wash from her hands. She confesses to encouraging Macbeth to kill Duncan and refers to Banquo's death as well. She is obsessed with the blood on her hands and she is unable to wash it off. She exclaims, "Out damn spot" as she unsuccessfully tries to remove the blood from her hands. This shows the demise of Lady Macbeth. Her actions and the actions of Macbeth have caused her to loose her mind. The guilt she feels can no longer be controlled; she has lost control of herself.

Macbeth feels confident that he will be safe in battle because of the Witches' prophecy. Macbeth is so self-absorbed with the impending battle that when the Doctor informs him that he cannot help Lady Macbeth, Macbeth simply becomes angry and insists that the Doctor find a cure for her. He then dismisses the doctor and dresses for battle. Macbeth is detached from reality and unaware of the severe condition of his wife. He is so consumed with rage and lust for power that his own wife is no longer important to him. The Witches are the only other source besides himself that Macbeth can trust. He must remain in control at all costs; even if he must spill more blood.

Malcolm and his men ready themselves for battle by using branches from Birnam Wood to shield themselves while approaching Dunsinane. In this way, the Witches' prophecy is fulfilled. Macbeth is informed that Lady Macbeth is dead; he does not even ask how she died. He is only concerned about himself and guarding his power. When the Messenger informs Macbeth that trees seem to be moving toward the castle, Macbeth is angered with him. However, he soon realizes that the Witches' prophecy is coming to pass. His response is to face the battle even if it means his death.

Macbeth has false hopes in his battle with Young Siward because he feels he cannot be harmed by any woman born of man. After Macbeth kills Young Siward, he feels even more confident that he is immortal. He feels he cannot be harmed and will remain in power because of his prophecy.

Macduff faces Macbeth filled with rage and vengeance. When he tells Macbeth that he was "untimely ripped" from his mother's womb, Macbeth realizes that the Witches gave him information that had a double meaning. Macbeth at that moment realizes that his fate has been sealed and he is not immortal.

Macbeth and Macduff fight. They disappear offstage, then return still fighting. Macbeth is then slain and Macduff carries his body offstage. By having the fight momentarily disapear offstage, the drama builds as the audience anticipates the outcome. Since Shakespeare did not have the benefits of modern moviemaking, Macbeth's body had to be taken offstage in order for Macduff to return with the severed head.

The play concludes with Malcom being restored to his rightful place on the throne.

Macbeth is a tragic hero because he has the potential for greatness, but it is undercut by his greed and lust for power. The prophecies of the Witches provide the spark by which Macbeth's soul is set on fire. Once he is presented with the chance to further his own ambition, he lets nothing and no one get in his way. Loyalty becomes treachery and friends become enemies. Even Lady Macbeth's death is naught but a nuisance. Macbeth tells Seyton that she should have waited until tomorrow to die because then he could have spent time mourning for her.

Shakespeare knew how to interpret the complex forces which drive men. On one level, *Macbeth* is about the fight between good and evil. Yet, it is told from the perspective of one man, Macbeth. Even within his own mind, Macbeth is torn between what is right (supporting Duncan) and what is wrong (following his own ambition). Macbeth is not a one dimensional character. He is not wholly evil, there are patches of goodness and regret within him. It is this intricate portrait of Macbeth's personality which adds realism to a play with such supernatural overtones.

Macbeth's road to ruin is twisted and branching. He is offered chances to reverse his course and save himself, but he sticks to the path of personal ambition. Each murderous act leads to another, more horrific than the last. The Witches are often blamed for Macbeth's downfall because he would not have killed the King if he had not heard tales of the future. But, Macbeth does not begin to plan the murder of Duncan until after Malcolm has been named successor. Until that point, Macbeth would have been proclaimed King had Duncan died according to Scottish law. Duncan's announcement usurps that law and Macbeth begins his bloody quest.

In the end, the play has come full circle. At the beginning, Macbeth defends the King against those who would overthrow the crown. In the end Macbeth, who has taken the crown by blood and deceit, is overthrown and rightful rule is restored.

Study Questions

1. What does the Doctor say to Macbeth about Lady Macbeth's condition? What is Macbeth's reaction?

2. What is the Doctor referring to when he says, "Therein the patient Must minister to himself?"

3. What does the Messenger tell Macbeth he sees coming toward Dunsinane? How does Macbeth respond?

4. What does Macduff vow to do to Macbeth and why? Cite an example from Act V.

5. What difference can you cite between Macbeth's army and Malcolm's army?

6. Whom does Macbeth kill in Act V? Do you feel that is important? State your reasons.

7. What does Macbeth say to Macduff about his mortality? What is Macduff's response? How does Macbeth react?

8. What does Ross tell Siward about Siward's son?

9. What does Malcolm say about Macbeth and Lady Macbeth?

10. What title has never been used before in Scotland that Malcolm plans to use on his Thanes and kinsman?

Answers

1. The Doctor says Lady Macbeth is very ill and he cannot cure her himself. Macbeth is angry and does not want to be bothered with this information.

2. The Doctor is saying that Macbeth is trying to tell the doctor how to cure his patient, Lady Macbeth. When in fact Macbeth is the patient himself.

3. The Messenger tells Macbeth that trees are moving toward the castle. Macbeth does not believe him at first; then, sounds the alarm for battle.

4. Macduff vows to have revenge on Macbeth because of the death of his family.

5. Malcolm's army if committed to the cause of saving Scotland. Macbeth's army is fighting for him out of fear they will be killed themselves.

6. Macbeth kills Young Siward. Answers may vary on the response to the second part of the question. The importance of the murder is seen in Macbeth's response after the murder. He states he cannot be killed by a man born of woman. He feels he cannot be harmed.

7. Macbeth tells Macduff that he cannot be harmed by man born of woman. Macduff tells Macbeth that he was ripped from his mother's womb. Macbeth realizes that the Witches have tricked him.

8. Ross tells Siward that his son was killed in battle.

9. Malcolm says that Macbeth is a "butcher" and Lady Macbeth was a "fiend-like queen". He also says that Lady Macbeth took her own life.

10. Malcolm plans to make the Thanes and kinsman Earls.

Suggested Essay Topics

1. Describe Macbeth's reaction to Lady Macbeth's death. Compare his reaction to the reaction he had after the murder of Duncan.

2. Elaborate on the importance of the scene when Lady Macbeth says, "Out damned spot! out, I say! One; two. Why then 'tis time to do't. Hell is murky. Fie, my lord, fie! a soldier, and afeard? What need we fear who knows it, when none can call our pow'r to accompt? Yet who would have thought the old man to have had so much blood in him?" This scene illustrates a change in the character of Lady Macbeth?

Bibliography

Adventures in English Literature. Shakespeare, William, "Macbeth." Orlando, Florida: Harcourt Brace Jovanovich, 1985.

Boyce, Charles. *Shakespeare A to Z*; New York: Roundtable Press, Inc., 1990.

Goddard, Howard C. *The Meaning of Shakespeare*. Chicago: University of Chicago Press, 1951.

Schmidt, Alexander. *Shakespeare Lexicon and Quotation Dictionary*; Vol. I and II. New York: Dover, 1971.

Taylor, Gary. *Reinventing Shakespeare. New York: Oxford University Press, 1989.*

DOVER · THRIFT · EDITIONS

FICTION

ADVENTURES OF HUCKLEBERRY FINN, Mark Twain. (0-486-28061-6)

THE AWAKENING, Kate Chopin. (0-486-27786-0)

A CHRISTMAS CAROL, Charles Dickens. (0-486-26865-9)

FRANKENSTEIN, Mary Shelley. (0-486-28211-2)

HEART OF DARKNESS, Joseph Conrad. (0-486-26464-5)

PRIDE AND PREJUDICE, Jane Austen. (0-486-28473-5)

THE SCARLET LETTER, Nathaniel Hawthorne. (0-486-28048-9)

THE ADVENTURES OF TOM SAWYER, Mark Twain. (0-486-40077-8)

ALICE'S ADVENTURES IN WONDERLAND, Lewis Carroll. (0-486-27543-4)

THE CALL OF THE WILD, Jack London. (0-486-26472-6)

CRIME AND PUNISHMENT, Fyodor Dostoyevsky. Translated by Constance Garnett. (0-486-41587-2)

DRACULA, Bram Stoker. (0-486-41109-5)

ETHAN FROME, Edith Wharton. (0-486-26690-7)

FLATLAND, Edwin A. Abbott. (0-486-27263-X)

GREAT AMERICAN SHORT STORIES, Edited by Paul Negri. (0-486-42119-8)

GREAT EXPECTATIONS, Charles Dickens. (0-486-41586-4)

JANE EYRE, Charlotte Brontë. (0-486-42449-9)

THE JUNGLE, Upton Sinclair. (0-486-41923-1)

THE METAMORPHOSIS AND OTHER STORIES, Franz Kafka. (0-486-29030-1)

THE ODYSSEY, Homer. (0-486-40654-7)

THE PICTURE OF DORIAN GRAY, Oscar Wilde. (0-486-27807-7)

SIDDHARTHA, Hermann Hesse. (0-486-40653-9)

THE STRANGE CASE OF DR. JEKYLL AND MR. HYDE, Robert Louis Stevenson. (0-486-26688-5)

A TALE OF TWO CITIES, Charles Dickens. (0-486-40651-2)

WUTHERING HEIGHTS, Emily Brontë. (0-486-29256-8)

ANNA KARENINA, Leo Tolstoy. Translated by Louise and Aylmer Maude. (0-486-43796-5)

AROUND THE WORLD IN EIGHTY DAYS, Jules Verne. (0-486-41111-7)

THE BROTHERS KARAMAZOV, Fyodor Dostoyevsky. Translated by Constance Garnett. (0-486-43791-4)

CANDIDE, Voltaire. Edited by Francois-Marie Arouet. (0-486-26689-3)

FICTION

DAISY MILLER, Henry James. (0-486-28773-4)

DAVID COPPERFIELD, Charles Dickens. (0-486-43665-9)

DUBLINERS, James Joyce. (0-486-26870-5)

EMMA, Jane Austen. (0-486-40648-2)

THE GIFT OF THE MAGI AND OTHER SHORT STORIES, O. Henry. (0-486-27061-0)

THE GOLD-BUG AND OTHER TALES, Edgar Allan Poe. (0-486-26875-6)

GREAT SHORT SHORT STORIES, Edited by Paul Negri. (0-486-44098-2)

GULLIVER'S TRAVELS, Jonathan Swift. (0-486-29273-8)

HARD TIMES, Charles Dickens. (0-486-41920-7)

THE HOUND OF THE BASKERVILLES, Arthur Conan Doyle. (0-486-28214-7)

THE ILIAD, Homer. (0-486-40883-3)

MOBY-DICK, Herman Melville. (0-486-43215-7)

MY ÁNTONIA, Willa Cather. (0-486-28240-6)

NORTHANGER ABBEY, Jane Austen. (0-486-41412-4)

NOT WITHOUT LAUGHTER, Langston Hughes. (0-486-45448-7)

OLIVER TWIST, Charles Dickens. (0-486-42453-7)

PERSUASION, Jane Austen. (0-486-29555-9)

THE PHANTOM OF THE OPERA, Gaston Leroux. (0-486-43458-3)

A PORTRAIT OF THE ARTIST AS A YOUNG MAN, James Joyce. (0-486-28050-0)

PUDD'NHEAD WILSON, Mark Twain. (0-486-40885-X)

THE RED BADGE OF COURAGE, Stephen Crane. (0-486-26465-3)

THE SCARLET PIMPERNEL, Baroness Orczy. (0-486-42122-8)

SENSE AND SENSIBILITY, Jane Austen. (0-486-29049-2)

SILAS MARNER, George Eliot. (0-486-29246-0)

TESS OF THE D'URBERVILLES, Thomas Hardy. (0-486-41589-9)

THE TIME MACHINE, H. G. Wells. (0-486-28472-7)

TREASURE ISLAND, Robert Louis Stevenson. (0-486-27559-0)

THE TURN OF THE SCREW, Henry James. (0-486-26684-2)

UNCLE TOM'S CABIN, Harriet Beecher Stowe. (0-486-44028-1)

THE WAR OF THE WORLDS, H. G. Wells. (0-486-29506-0)

THE WORLD'S GREATEST SHORT STORIES, Edited by James Daley. (0-486-44716-2)

THE AGE OF INNOCENCE, Edith Wharton. (0-486-29803-5)

DOVER · THRIFT · EDITIONS

FICTION

AGNES GREY, Anne Brontë. (0-486-45121-6)

AT FAULT, Kate Chopin. (0-486-46133-5)

THE AUTOBIOGRAPHY OF AN EX-COLORED MAN, James Weldon Johnson. (0-486-28512-X)

BARTLEBY AND BENITO CERENO, Herman Melville. (0-486-26473-4)

BEOWULF, Translated by R. K. Gordon. (0-486-27264-8)

CIVIL WAR STORIES, Ambrose Bierce. (0-486-28038-1)

A CONNECTICUT YANKEE IN KING ARTHUR'S COURT, Mark Twain. (0-486-41591-0)

THE DEERSLAYER, James Fenimore Cooper. (0-486-46136-X)

DEMIAN, Hermann Hesse. (0-486-41413-2)

FAR FROM THE MADDING CROWD, Thomas Hardy. (0-486-45684-6)

FAVORITE FATHER BROWN STORIES, G. K. Chesterton. (0-486-27545-0)

GREAT HORROR STORIES, Edited by John Grafton. Introduction by Mike Ashley. (0-486-46143-2)

GREAT RUSSIAN SHORT STORIES, Edited by Paul Negri. (0-486-42992-X)

GREAT SHORT STORIES BY AMERICAN WOMEN, Edited by Candace Ward. (0-486-28776-9)

GRIMM'S FAIRY TALES, Jacob and Wilhelm Grimm. (0-486-45656-0)

HUMOROUS STORIES AND SKETCHES, Mark Twain. (0-486-29279-7)

THE HUNCHBACK OF NOTRE DAME, Victor Hugo. Translated by A. L. Alger. (0-486-45242-5)

THE INVISIBLE MAN, H. G. Wells. (0-486-27071-8)

THE ISLAND OF DR. MOREAU, H. G. Wells. (0-486-29027-1)

A JOURNAL OF THE PLAGUE YEAR, Daniel Defoe. (0-486-41919-3)

JOURNEY TO THE CENTER OF THE EARTH, Jules Verne. (0-486-44088-5)

KIM, Rudyard Kipling. (0-486-44508-9)

THE LAST OF THE MOHICANS, James Fenimore Cooper. (0-486-42678-5)

THE LEGEND OF SLEEPY HOLLOW AND OTHER STORIES, Washington Irving. (0-486-46658-2)

LILACS AND OTHER STORIES, Kate Chopin. (0-486-44095-8)

MANSFIELD PARK, Jane Austen. (0-486-41585-6)

THE MAYOR OF CASTERBRIDGE, Thomas Hardy. (0-486-43749-3)

THE MYSTERIOUS STRANGER AND OTHER STORIES, Mark Twain. (0-486-27069-6)

NOTES FROM THE UNDERGROUND, Fyodor Dostoyevsky. (0-486-27053-X)

FICTION

O PIONEERS!, Willa Cather. (0-486-27785-2)

AN OCCURRENCE AT OWL CREEK BRIDGE AND OTHER STORIES, Ambrose Bierce. (0-486-46657-4)

THE OLD CURIOSITY SHOP, Charles Dickens. (0-486-42679-3)

THE OPEN BOAT AND OTHER STORIES, Stephen Crane. (0-486-27547-7)

ROBINSON CRUSOE, Daniel Defoe. (0-486-40427-7)

THIS SIDE OF PARADISE, F. Scott Fitzgerald. (0-486-28999-0)

THE THREE MUSKETEERS, Alexandre Dumas. (0-486-45681-1)

TWENTY THOUSAND LEAGUES UNDER THE SEA, Jules Verne. (0-486-44849-5)

WHITE FANG, Jack London. (0-486-26968-X)

WHITE NIGHTS AND OTHER STORIES, Fyodor Dostoyevsky. (0-486-46948-4)

NONFICTION

GREAT SPEECHES, Abraham Lincoln. (0-486-26872-1)

WISDOM OF THE BUDDHA, Edited by F. Max Müller. (0-486-41120-6)

NARRATIVE OF SOJOURNER TRUTH, Sojourner Truth. (0-486-29899-X)

THE TRIAL AND DEATH OF SOCRATES, Plato. (0-486-27066-1)

WIT AND WISDOM OF THE AMERICAN PRESIDENTS, Edited by Joslyn Pine. (0-486-41427-2)

GREAT SPEECHES BY AFRICAN AMERICANS, Edited by James Daley. (0-486-44761-8)

INTERIOR CASTLE, St. Teresa of Avila. Edited and Translated by E. Allison Peers. (0-486-46145-9)

GREAT SPEECHES BY AMERICAN WOMEN, Edited by James Daley. (0-486-46141-6)

ON LIBERTY, John Stuart Mill. (0-486-42130-9)

MEDITATIONS, Marcus Aurelius. (0-486-29823-X)

THE SOULS OF BLACK FOLK, W.E.B. DuBois. (0-486-28041-1)

GREAT SPEECHES BY NATIVE AMERICANS, Edited by Bob Blaisdell. (0-486-41122-2)

WIT AND WISDOM FROM POOR RICHARD'S ALMANACK, Benjamin Franklin. (0-486-40891-4)

THE AUTOBIOGRAPHY OF BENJAMIN FRANKLIN, Benjamin Franklin. (0-486-29073-5)

OSCAR WILDE'S WIT AND WISDOM, Oscar Wilde. (0-486-40146-4)

THE WIT AND WISDOM OF ABRAHAM LINCOLN, Abraham Lincoln. Edited by Bob Blaisdell. (0-486-44097-4)

DOVER · THRIFT · EDITIONS

NONFICTION

ON THE ORIGIN OF SPECIES, Charles Darwin. (0-486-45006-6)

SIX GREAT DIALOGUES, Plato. Translated by Benjamin Jowett. (0-486-45465-7)

NATURE AND OTHER ESSAYS, Ralph Waldo Emerson. (0-486-46947-6)

THE COMMUNIST MANIFESTO AND OTHER REVOLUTIONARY WRITINGS, Edited by Bob Blaisdell. (0-486-42465-0)

THE CONFESSIONS OF ST. AUGUSTINE, St. Augustine. (0-486-42466-9)

THE WIT AND WISDOM OF MARK TWAIN, Mark Twain. (0-486-40664-4)

LIFE ON THE MISSISSIPPI, Mark Twain. (0-486-41426-4)

BEYOND GOOD AND EVIL, Friedrich Nietzsche. (0-486-29868-X)

CIVIL DISOBEDIENCE AND OTHER ESSAYS, Henry David Thoreau. (0-486-27563-9)

A MODEST PROPOSAL AND OTHER SATIRICAL WORKS, Jonathan Swift. (0-486-28759-9)

UTOPIA, Sir Thomas More. (0-486-29583-4)

GREAT SPEECHES, Franklin Delano Roosevelt. (0-486-40894-9)

WALDEN; OR, LIFE IN THE WOODS, Henry David Thoreau. (0-486-28495-6)

UP FROM SLAVERY, Booker T. Washington. (0-486-28738-6)

DARK NIGHT OF THE SOUL, St. John of the Cross. (0-486-42693-9)

GREEK AND ROMAN LIVES, Plutarch. Translated by John Dryden. Revised and Edited by Arthur Hugh Clough. (0-486-44576-3)

WOMEN'S WIT AND WISDOM, Edited by Susan L. Rattiner. (0-486-41123-0)

MUSIC, Edited by Herb Galewitz. (0-486-41596-1)

INCIDENTS IN THE LIFE OF A SLAVE GIRL, Harriet Jacobs. (0-486-41931-2)

THE LIFE OF OLAUDAH EQUIANO, Olaudah Equiano. (0-486-40661-X)

THE DECLARATION OF INDEPENDENCE AND OTHER GREAT DOCUMENTS OF AMERICAN HISTORY, Edited by John Grafton. (0-486-41124-9)

THE PRINCE, Niccolò Machiavelli. (0-486-27274-5)

WOMAN IN THE NINETEENTH CENTURY, Margaret Fuller. (0-486-40662-8)

SELF-RELIANCE AND OTHER ESSAYS, Ralph Waldo Emerson. (0-486-27790-9)

COMMON SENSE, Thomas Paine. (0-486-29602-4)

THE REPUBLIC, Plato. (0-486-41121-4)

POETICS, Aristotle. (0-486-29577-X)

THE DEVIL'S DICTIONARY, Ambrose Bierce. (0-486-27542-6)

NARRATIVE OF THE LIFE OF FREDERICK DOUGLASS, Frederick Douglass. (0-486-28499-9)

DOVER · THRIFT · EDITIONS

NONFICTION

GREAT ENGLISH ESSAYS, Edited by Bob Blaisdell. (0-486-44082-6)

THE KORAN, Translated by J. M. Rodwell. (0-486-44569-0)

28 GREAT INAUGURAL ADDRESSES, Edited by John Grafton and James Daley. (0-486-44621-2)

WHEN I WAS A SLAVE, Edited by Norman R. Yetman. (0-486-42070-1)

THE IMITATION OF CHRIST, Thomas à Kempis. Translated by Aloysius Croft and Harold Bolton. (0-486-43185-1)

PLAYS

ANTIGONE, Sophocles. (0-486-27804-2)

AS YOU LIKE IT, William Shakespeare. (0-486-40432-3)

CYRANO DE BERGERAC, Edmond Rostand. (0-486-41119-2)

A DOLL'S HOUSE, Henrik Ibsen. (0-486-27062-9)

DR. FAUSTUS, Christopher Marlowe. (0-486-28208-2)

FIVE COMIC ONE-ACT PLAYS, Anton Chekhov. (0-486-40887-6)

FIVE GREAT COMEDIES, William Shakespeare. (0-486-44086-9)

FIVE GREAT GREEK TRAGEDIES, Sophocles, Euripides and Aeschylus. (0-486-43620-9)

FOUR GREAT HISTORIES, William Shakespeare. (0-486-44629-8)

FOUR GREAT RUSSIAN PLAYS, Anton Chekhov, Nikolai Gogol, Maxim Gorky, and Ivan Turgenev. (0-486-43472-9)

FOUR GREAT TRAGEDIES, William Shakespeare. (0-486-44083-4)

GHOSTS, Henrik Ibsen. (0-486-29852-3)

HAMLET, William Shakespeare. (0-486-27278-8)

HENRY V, William Shakespeare. (0-486-42887-7)

AN IDEAL HUSBAND, Oscar Wilde. (0-486-41423-X)

THE IMPORTANCE OF BEING EARNEST, Oscar Wilde. (0-486-26478-5)

JULIUS CAESAR, William Shakespeare. (0-486-26876-4)

KING LEAR, William Shakespeare. (0-486-28058-6)

LOVE'S LABOUR'S LOST, William Shakespeare. (0-486-41929-0)

LYSISTRATA, Aristophanes. (0-486-28225-2)

MACBETH, William Shakespeare. (0-486-27802-6)

MAJOR BARBARA, George Bernard Shaw. (0-486-42126-0)

MEDEA, Euripides. (0-486-27548-5)

DOVER · THRIFT · EDITIONS

PLAYS

THE MERCHANT OF VENICE, William Shakespeare. (0-486-28492-1)

A MIDSUMMER NIGHT'S DREAM, William Shakespeare. (0-486-27067-X)

MUCH ADO ABOUT NOTHING, William Shakespeare. (0-486-28272-4)

OEDIPUS REX, Sophocles. (0-486-26877-2)

THE ORESTEIA TRILOGY, Aeschylus. (0-486-29242-8)

OTHELLO, William Shakespeare. (0-486-29097-2)

THE PLAYBOY OF THE WESTERN WORLD AND RIDERS TO THE SEA, J. M. Synge. (0-486-27562-0)

PYGMALION, George Bernard Shaw. (0-486-28222-8)

ROMEO AND JULIET, William Shakespeare. (0-486-27557-4)

THE TAMING OF THE SHREW, William Shakespeare. (0-486-29765-9)

TARTUFFE, Molière. (0-486-41117-6)

THE TEMPEST, William Shakespeare. (0-486-40658-X)

TWELFTH NIGHT; OR, WHAT YOU WILL, William Shakespeare. (0-486-29290-8)

RICHARD III, William Shakespeare. (0-486-28747-5)

HEDDA GABLER, Henrik Ibsen. (0-486-26469-6)

THE COMEDY OF ERRORS, William Shakespeare. (0-486-42461-8)

THE CHERRY ORCHARD, Anton Chekhov. (0-486-26682-6)

SHE STOOPS TO CONQUER, Oliver Goldsmith. (0-486-26867-5)

THE WILD DUCK, Henrik Ibsen. (0-486-41116-8)

THE WINTER'S TALE, William Shakespeare. (0-486-41118-4)

ARMS AND THE MAN, George Bernard Shaw. (0-486-26476-9)

EVERYMAN, Anonymous. (0-486-28726-2)

THE FATHER, August Strindberg. (0-486-43217-3)

R.U.R., Karel Capek. (0-486-41926-6)

THE BEGGAR'S OPERA, John Gay. (0-486-40888-4)

3 BY SHAKESPEARE, William Shakespeare. (0-486-44721-9)

PROMETHEUS BOUND, Aeschylus. (0-486-28762-9)

REA's Study Guides

Review Books, Refreshers, and Comprehensive References

Problem Solvers®

Presenting an answer to the pressing need for easy-to-understand and up-to-date study guides detailing the wide world of mathematics and science.

High School Tutors®

In-depth guides that cover the length and breadth of the science and math subjects taught in high schools nationwide.

Essentials®

An insightful series of more useful, more practical, and more informative references comprehensively covering more than 150 subjects.

Super Reviews®

Don't miss a thing! Review it all thoroughly with this series of complete subject references at an affordable price.

Interactive Flashcard Books®

Flip through these essential, interactive study aids that go far beyond ordinary flashcards.

Reference

Explore dozens of clearly written, practical guides covering a wide scope of subjects from business to engineering to languages and many more.

For information about any of REA's books, visit
www.rea.com

Research & Education Association
61 Ethel Road W., Piscataway, NJ 08854
Phone: (732) 819-8880